James Moloney lives in Brisbane with his wife, two teenage daughters, a son and a dog who drives him nuts. He has worked as an art union ticket seller, a gopher at a wholesale fruit market and a teacher. These days he devotes most of his time to what he loves best — writing books for young people, two of which have won the Australian Children's Book of the Year Award, *Swashbuckler* in 1996 and *A Bridge to Wiseman's Cove* in 1997. Of *Black Taxi*, he says, 'If people have as much fun reading it as I had writing it, we'll all have to take Monday off to get over it.'

Black Taxi was shortlisted for the 2004 Adelaide Festival Children's Literature Award and the 2004 Children's Book Council Award for Older Readers.

'A delightful and funny crime/adventure romp'
Agnes Nieuwenhuisen, July 2003

'*Black Taxi* bubbles along ... never missing a beat, never running out of fuel'
Magpies magazine, July 2003

JAMES MOLONEY
BLACK TAXI

Angus&Robertson
An imprint of HarperCollins*Publishers*

Angus&Robertson
An imprint of HarperCollins*Publishers*

First published in Australia in 2003
by HarperCollins*Publishers* Pty Limited
ABN 36 009 913 517
A member of the HarperCollins*Publishers* (Australia) Pty Limited Group
www.harpercollins.com.au

HarperCollins*Publishers*
25 Ryde Road, Pymble, Sydney NSW 2073, Australia
31 View Road, Glenfield, Auckland 10, New Zealand
77–85 Fulham Palace Road, London W6 8JB, United Kingdom
2 Bloor Street East, 20th floor, Toronto, Ontario M4W 1A8, Canada
10 East 53rd Street, New York NY 10022, USA

National Library of Australia Cataloguing-in-publication data:

Moloney, James.
    For teenagers aged 13+.
    ISBN 0 2071 9989 2.
    1. Teenage girls – Juvenile fiction. 2. Family – Juvenile fiction. I. Title.
A823.3

Designed by Lore Foye and Alys Martin, HarperCollins Design Studio
Printed and bound in Australia by Griffin Press on 60gsm Bulky Paperback

5 4 3 2   04 05 06

For my daughter Siobhan

ONE

PADDY LARKIN IS JUST A little bent. I don't mean he's one of those wrinklies you see walking along the street all doubled over like an upside down 'L'. I mean he doesn't always stick to the straight and narrow. To put it bluntly, Patrick Larkin is a crook.

But he's a nice crook, and he wouldn't hurt a mouse. He also happens to be my grandfather. He likes me and I like him. Maybe that's obvious already. Once, when I was fourteen and starting to bulge in new directions, he said, 'Rosie, you're like a race track in a young man's dreams. Lots of tight curves.'

He was smiling when he said it and he gave me a hug, a real grandfather's hug that showed how much

1

he loved me. 'Any boy who breaks your heart had better watch out,' he added solemnly. That didn't stop them, but it was great to know I had a grandfather who would look out for me.

Paddy has been more like a father than a grandfather. As for my real father, hell, I haven't seen him for ... to tell you the truth, I don't remember, and I certainly don't care. All he ever gave me was a surname. Sinclair.

It was Grandad who taught me how to drive, in his own car, too, the Mercedes he loves so much, the one he bought from the funeral home when it went bust. (How a funeral home could go bankrupt when there are always people dying is something I never quite worked out.)

Actually, the way he snaffled that car says a lot about Paddy Larkin. He went to the auction of all the funeral gear just to see what was there, along with everyone else in Prestwidge — a sort of outing for the curious. There was the Mercedes Benz, a 280 S, one of those classic styles from the 1960s, and as soon as he saw it, he fell in love. 'It's my one chance to have something special,' he told Grandma. Perfect condition, too. After all, who's in a hurry to arrive at the cemetery?

There were a few others taking a close look at the Merc that day, so Grandad dropped a word here and there about why the funeral home had gone out of business. 'Disrespect for the dead,' he whispered with a knowing smile and tap on his nose as though he knew all about it. 'When the hearse was too busy to pick up a new corpse, they'd use this Mercedes, eh.' He'd seen it with someone's feet sticking out one of the back windows, he told them.

There was also a pair of roof racks in the auction. Grandad spread the word that they were kept in the boot of the Mercedes, and that when there was no room in the back seat they'd strap a body to the top of the car. 'Like a surfboard,' he said, showing them his arm held rigid from elbow to fingertip. 'It helped if they were already stiff, of course.'

When the bidding started, no-one seem very interested in that black Mercedes. The auctioneer just couldn't work it out. Then Grandad put up his hand and the car was his. 'Just business,' he told me afterwards. Who am I to argue? I love driving it.

I had to drive it on a Monday morning recently, to an event as sad as any funeral. We were taking Grandad to court. Despite all his clever wiles, Paddy Larkin had been arrested again. The first time he went up before a judge, years ago, the magistrate had thrown the case out because the idiot cops had made a mess of the evidence. Mind you, the cops, the judge, the solicitor and especially our family knew Grandad was guilty as.

Then he got done fair and square with three cartons of thermal underwear in the boot of the Mercedes and another two in the back seat, but the judge said he'd suspend the sentence since it was Grandad's first offence.

First offence! Ha! First time they could prove it, that was all.

But now he'd been picked up a third time and the judge had lost patience. So Grandad looked like he was going to gaol. In fact, his solicitor was pretty sure he would get six months. He could probably do with the rest, considering how much he does around Prestwidge to help people out. (I was about to find out *exactly* how much.) In fact, if there was one reason why the whole thing was unfair on my poor grandad, it was because he had only got caught because he was doing a good turn, in this case for Uncle Bruce. That's Uncle Bruce the Slimeball. Oh, don't get me started.

Uncle Bruce was sitting beside me as I drove the Mercedes that Monday morning. Behind us in the back seat, I could see Grandad's big face in the mirror. It was leathery, with deep creases around the eyes and heavy eyebrows, thick and bushy. He was in the middle, with Grandma crying softly on one side of him and my mother having hysterics on the other.

We were 'his girls', as he called us — wife, daughter and granddaughter. It was Grandma I felt sorry for today. She must have been dreading that this day would come for a long time. She was dressed all in black, like one of those little Greek grandmothers you see round the streets sometimes. Bit odd, with a name like Larkin.

Grandma was a good match for Paddy. If he started going on about stupid politicians or the kids

4

who hang around the streets of Prestwidge looking for something to do, she would tell him to pull his head in. She was a wizard with a pack of cards, too. Mum and I could never tell what kind of a hand she was holding until WHAM, she would do us like a dinner. But today we definitely weren't seeing her at her best.

Grandad saw my eyes in the little frame of the mirror and smiled. 'Eyes on the road, Rosie,' he said, somehow managing not to sound like a nag.

Normally he'd be driving it himself, but just as we were leaving, he tossed me the keys. 'I can't drive and take care of these two at the same time,' he whispered in my ear. So I was the chauffeur.

I'd only been asked along in the first place so there would be someone to drive the car back again afterwards. Grandad himself would probably have to stay behind with the cops. (Oops, not thinking about that one.) And Uncle Bruce had lost his licence for drink driving. Second time, too. If he's caught again it will probably be him off to gaol as well. Once he's driving again, I'm going to have a good sniff every time he comes round to borrow money from Mum, and if there's booze on his breath, I'll phone the police and dob him in. That sounds cruel, but if you're waiting for me to take it back you'd better find a comfortable place to sit.

That left the women, but Grandma was prone to fainting spells, including the one she had while she was behind the wheel of this precious Mercedes.

Luckily, neither Grandma nor the car was damaged. As for Mum, well, it's usually her passengers who faint.

My mother Cynthia Sinclair is the only person in the history of Prestwidge to have had two accidents in the same driving test. Both happened while she was trying for a reverse park. She managed to go all the way back into the car behind her and then come forward into the car in front. 'Just making the space big enough, eh!' the policeman told his mates back at the station, laughing his head off. She passed a year later at the fourth attempt, and ever since then the people of Prestwidge have kept off the roads on Thursday nights around seven o'clock, which is when Mum goes down to Woolworths to do the weekly shopping.

My mother's hairdressing salon is called Hair by Sinclair, which says a lot about her taste and imagination. Luckily, we aren't the least bit alike. My hair is black. Hers is orange. I *have* never and *will* never wear a leopard-skin print. Mum has a leopard-skin skirt, and worse, matching shoes. The skirt is too short and the heels are too high. Really, old women should know when to give up. She is forty-three years old, for God's sake! I saw a picture of her once when she was eighteen and she didn't look too bad, but now she's got an eighteen-year-old daughter of her own.

Grandad loves her anyway, but I know he shares my opinion about her driving ability, so if there is one certainty in life, it's that she is never going to drive his car. So I was called in, even though I had to take the day off school. Real trouble shooter, that's me. Anyway, it was Monday, and my timetable is a shocker.

I should have already finished Year Twelve by now … long story. The shortened version is that I left after Year Ten to be Mum's apprentice at Hair by Sinclair. Twelve months of looking at my mother wearing leopard skin day and night was enough to make my Prestwidge High School uniform look like an Yves Saint Laurent. So I went back to do Year Eleven and Twelve and now I've got just one semester to go. Then I really *will* be finished with school.

But on to the courtroom. We'd just crossed the bridge leading into the city centre when the matter came up. 'So who's going to have this car while you're inside?' asked Uncle Bruce.

See how his mind works? He didn't even give a damn about his own father. He was already looking for the main chance, and this after Grandad had been caught flogging that stuff for *him*.

'The car?' whispered Grandad. I guess when you're heading for gaol, some details can slip your mind. He was worried about Grandma, of course. The fainting fits meant she couldn't live on her own, so just yesterday we had agreed that she would come and live with us. But the car?

'I don't know,' he mumbled. 'It will have to stay shut up in the garage at home, I suppose.'

Uncle Bruce saw his chance. 'It'll need a run every now and then so the battery doesn't go flat. Tell you what, I'll pop round every week and rev it up for you.' I swear his voice sounded like he was doing Grandad a favour.

'But you've lost your licence.'

'Don't need a licence just to start it up in the garage.'

'How are you going to get to our place when you can't drive?'

Bruce looked thoughtful, as though he were genuinely hunting around for a solution when in fact he had it all worked out. 'I know. The Merc can stay in *my* garage.'

'There'll be plenty of room,' I said maliciously. Bruce had been forced to sell his clapped-out old bomb to pay the drink-driving fine.

Grandad wasn't falling for this scam. 'You'd drive it all over the place. Use it like it was your own and before you know it they'd nab you for driving without a licence.'

'I won't get caught. You don't have to carry round a flashing sign that says *Disqualified Driver*.' He made flicking movements with his fingers, like he was a neon sign.

'How would you pay the fine? They'd impound the car and sell it out from under me.'

'I'm telling you, I won't get caught.'

'NO,' said Grandad firmly. No-one can say 'NO' quite like Paddy Larkin.

The car went quiet for a minute or two. Then my mother piped up. 'Jason needs a car.'

Grandad looked at her; Grandma stopped crying and looked at her. Uncle Bruce turned right round in the front seat to glare at her. I tell you, if I hadn't been watching the road, I'd have turned round to stare at her too.

'What's the matter with you lot?' said Mum, when she found all those eyes boring into her. 'At least Jason's got a licence.'

Grandad snorted, as he does now and again when he is thoroughly disgusted. 'He's got an empty head, that's what he's got. I don't like to speak ill of my own grandson, Cynthia, but he needs a good kick up the arse.' Grandma nudged him in the ribs. 'Sorry. Didn't mean to swear.'

'You sound like those mongrels down at Centrelink. They've cut off his unemployment again, you know. What do they expect, sending him along to that chook factory for a job? It was an insult. I mean, he finished Year Twelve, didn't he? If he had a car for a while, he might make something of himself.'

Ha! The only thing my brother Jason is ever likely to make of himself is a stretch of carpet. I've seen slugs with more get-up-and-go. He lives at home with Mum and me. Actually, he lives on the sofa in the lounge room, just like one of the cushions. Half the time he doesn't even bother going to bed. I throw a blanket over him sometimes, and if Mum didn't bring him food he would be a skeleton by now.

Needless to say, he couldn't be bothered coming in to court today with the rest of us.

The others were still staring at Mum in heated disbelief. 'He just needs a chance,' she said lamely. I doubt she even believed it herself.

'NO,' said Grandad.

'Well, I guess it's up to me then,' said Mum. 'I'll come over once a week and take it round the block.'

A look of absolute horror passed over my grandfather's face. 'No, Cynthia. It'll be all right.' He had to think quickly. He saw me. 'Rosie. Rosie can do it.' Phew! He had saved the day. I saw him smile broadly in the rear-view mirror and grinned back at him. I love you, Grandad.

I was heading into the car park under the court building by now. I don't know what was happening to Grandad's stomach, but mine was tying itself into every knot in the Boy Scout handbook.

Just as I pulled up next to a brand-new Mercedes that didn't look half as stylish as ours, Grandad spoke again. 'Rosie, you're a sensible girl and a bloody good driver. How long have you had your licence now?'

'Nearly a year, Grandad.'

'No accidents?'

'Not one.' (Well … but this was hardly the time to mention the little scratch I'd added to Mum's car. With so many already, she hadn't noticed it herself.)

'That's it, then. You can take care of the Mercedes while I'm away. Keep it at your place. You can even drive it around a bit if you like.'

And that was it. How to get a Mercedes without lifting a finger.

But if I'd known then what I know now, I'd have said no, with a Paddy Larkin firmness.

TWO

THINGS DIDN'T GO SO WELL in the courtroom that day. In fact, they went as badly as the solicitor expected. The case was really divided into what the police could prove (which looked bad for Grandad) and what they didn't even know (which was good for Uncle Bruce).

I knew the full story, and I constantly had to stop myself from jumping up in my place and shouting the truth to the judge and the prosecutor and the jury. If there had been the least chance of getting Grandad off that way, I would have done it, too. *Bruce is the one you want,* I would have told them. *Paddy doesn't do it any more. For God's sake, Paddy Larkin is RETIRED!*

Mind you, it had been quite a career. He didn't steal the stuff himself very often. His usual game was to take a batch of stolen goods — clothing or electrical items like videos — from the real thief, and to shift them quietly around to people who ran a flea-market stall or a second-hand shop. He thought of himself as more of a distributor. It's called 'redistribution of wealth'. We learned about it at school. He had his own circle of customers who trusted him because he was careful. Paddy Larkin was the someone who could get you things on the cheap, particularly if you were hard up. A real humanitarian, a caring bloke, that's my grandad, and I mean what I say.

But now he's retired. It was Bruce who forced him back into it, just for one last go. Bruce had 'acquired' a load of clothing, but no-one would buy it from him. He couldn't shift it, and it looked a bit incriminating sitting in his lounge room if the police ever called, which they did occasionally because they knew he was a slimeball as much as I did.

Grandad told him to dump it, but he wouldn't. He'd borrowed money from a loan shark to get hold of the stuff in the first place and he had to make good on the deal. So against his better judgment, Paddy agreed to help.

He went round to GG's — that's the nickname of his mate George Goggin, who has a van big enough to hold all the junk in Bruce's living room. Together Paddy and Bruce made the rounds of his usual customers. They unloaded all of it except for three parkas, which Paddy kept back for some old people he knew who were having a hard time. He dropped Uncle Bruce off at the pub, but on his way to deliver the van back to GG's the police pulled him over.

Dumb bad luck, it was. They were stopping every car in the area looking for someone else, but of course when they found Paddy driving a van, they did a search.

And what did they find? Three parkas, all the same, all brand-new and none of them Paddy's size. Even then, he might have talked his way out of it if Constable Enright hadn't been there. Who do you think had done the police report on the stolen clothing? In fact, he had been typing up the list of stolen goods in his own plodding, two-fingered style only an hour beforehand. He recognised the parkas, one thing led to another, and that's why we'd all ended up in a courtroom with Grandma crying quietly and my mother going off like a fire engine.

The jury did its job. Guilty.

Grandad stood before the judge. Six months, as expected.

We were given a few moments to say goodbye. Grandad went through his pockets. The wallet went to Grandma. When he saw me jingling the car keys miserably, he patted his coat pockets and found one last thing. 'Here, if you're minding the car, Rosie, you'd better take this.' He handed me his mobile phone. It was a little Nokia, brand new. Just as well the police didn't ask where he'd got it from. 'Look, a few people might call you, to run an errand or two.'

I gave him a worried look.

'Nothing illegal. I promise. Just driving people around.'

That was what he said. Honestly. Just driving people around.

Ha!

Problem: how to keep Grandad's car away from Uncle Bruce. I did have to go to school the next day, after all. If I miss more than a day at a time they tend to notice. Mum is at her salon all day, ensuring that every woman in Prestwidge has exactly the same hair style, a quest to which she has devoted her entire life.

Bruce lives a ten-minute drive away. With no car and no licence, he couldn't drive here, but if he had a friend that wouldn't be a problem. Luckily, he hasn't got any friends. He hasn't got a wife these days either, since the poor thing finally came to her senses last year and walked out, taking most of the furniture with her. Just backed a truck up to the front door, paid two apes to cart the stuff out for her and that was that. (The story goes that she left the dog's basket in the middle of the bedroom with a note suggesting he sleep in it. She left the dog, too. It's a red setter, crossbred with a barn door. Couldn't get a feed in a butcher's shop. The dog and Bruce are made for each other.)

But if Bruce is stupid in some ways, he is cunning in others — in fact, downright intelligent when he applies himself. He will get here one way or another, and if I leave the Mercedes in our garage, I may as well leave the keys in the ignition. Hot-wiring a car is one of his small repertoire of practical skills.

There was only one solution. I would have to drive the Mercedes to school and leave it in the teachers' car park. There have been so many thefts from the teachers' car park in recent years that they now lock the gates between nine and three.

I was almost there when the phone rang. I'd forgotten all about it. Popped it in the glove box when we left the courthouse, and it was still there, still turned on. The glove box was too far away for me to reach it while I was driving. Let it ring out, I decided.

The noise stopped, then seconds later started up again, muffled by all the other junk I'd seen in there. Was it for me? Well, all right. It sounds a bit ridiculous, but there's something about a ringing phone. It's a girl thing, maybe. I pulled over and reached into the glove box. 'Hello?'

'Who's this?'

'It's Rosie Sinclair.'

'Where's Paddy?'

'In gaol.'

'Shit!'

The phone went dead. I guess he didn't want to talk. That's a boy thing.

On to the teachers' car park. There's only one other student with a car at Prestwidge High School. Garret Hemmings has rich parents, and you'd expect him to be at a private school in the city somewhere. Well, he had been. He had tried out three of them and got himself expelled from each one. Around Prestwidge, though, he's no more of a bad boy than half a dozen others I could name. I think that came as a shock to Garret, and nowadays he contents himself with the occasional outburst of colourful language at selected teachers. So what else is new? If that could get you expelled from Prestwidge, half the classrooms would be empty.

As I locked the Mercedes, I looked up. Josh Willmot was staring at me from twenty metres away. He took off quickly, and by the time I reached the schoolyard the entire school knew.

'Where did you get it?'

'Who does it belong to?'

'Is it yours?'

'What kind of car is it?' This last question was greeted with a rolling of eyes and a collective sigh of 'Derrrr!'

'It's my grandad's. He's letting me drive it for a while.'

'Oh, where's he gone?' asked Rebecca Drake, as though she didn't know already. She had her ear to the ground for gossip more than almost anyone. I'm not a violent person (normally), but if she didn't watch out, one day I'd stomp on that ear — and the rest of her head, for that matter. Luckily for her, none of the other kids took up her hint.

Just then, the A List turned up. Justine, Clare and Fiona. Justine was six feet tall and already acted like the model she wanted to be. 'Wow, a car,' she gushed when Josh told her, 'and not just any car. A Mercedes.'

'It's pretty old,' someone pointed out, but the A List ignored this. I was suddenly in the loop. With so much happening so quickly, I hadn't counted on the attention Grandad's car would bring me — and I certainly hadn't anticipated a blossoming friendship with the likes of these three.

They were certainly *cool*. Hair just right, uniforms tweaked to follow the latest fashion trends. All the other girls were desperate to win their approval. Secretly, I suppose I was too, but old habits are hard to break. Before I went off for a year of sweeping hairy floors and learning to hate the smell of perming fluid, all this crowd were a year below me. And let's get real here: at school, anyone in the years below you is treated with contempt. Now they were my classmates, but I didn't always feel like fitting in.

My celebrity continued throughout morning tea. By lunch time, Justine and company had decided that I could have the privilege of driving them about. 'How about a ride?'

I know, I know. The answer should have been a Paddy Larkin 'NO.'

But what the heck. It was fun having the bold and the beautiful hanging about, wanting something from me. I was Paddy's granddaughter and I knew how the world worked. If I did something for these three, then I could ask for something in return. What exactly, I had no idea, but then that was half the fun.

'Where to?'

'Just up to The Grove.'

Oh, great. They wanted to do the movie star thing.

Allow me to explain. You see, Prestwidge doesn't really have a main street or a town centre. The only landmark that everyone knows is a huge white box of a building that seemed to fall from the sky at some point no-one can remember and land on hundreds of spindly little poles to create a car park underneath. This is the shopping centre grandly titled Prestwidge Grove. The locals quickly shortened it to The Grove.

Now for the movie star bit. In the greatest ever moment of Prestwidge's brief history, some ageing Hollywood name from Grandad's era turned up to open the new movie complex at The Grove. Red carpet, limos, the lot. These three airheads wanted me to deposit them on the same spot.

'OK,' I agreed.

After school, they were waiting for me, all three piling into the back seat. Where was my chauffeur's cap?

But if the Hollywood thing was their plan, it was quickly shoved into the boot when they spotted a figure in the street.

'Oh my God, it's Todd Rooney!'

It's impossible to describe adequately the pandemonium that accompanied this announcement. Squealing, shoving one another in the shoulder, jostling for the best vantage point when they were so tightly packed into the back seat. As for the dialogue that followed … no, I can't repeat it. Such turkey gobble is an insult to female intelligence.

All I glimpsed was a private school blazer hanging from a frame tall enough to look Justine in the eye when she was in her highest heels.

'He didn't see us!' Fiona wailed. 'Quick, Rosie. Go round the block.'

Yes, Ma'am. Who was I to spoil the fun?

The traffic was heavy, which made the girls even more agitated. 'Is he going to ask you out, Jus?' Clare demanded.

'*I* don't know,' she answered hotly. 'I've only spoken to him twice.'

'He's *so* hot!'

'What a hunk!'

'He's *gorgeous*!'

At least they were speaking in sentences again. The next step was to try for more than three words before the exclamation mark.

By now I had finally circumnavigated the huge shopping centre. Target dead ahead. The relief that he hadn't disappeared into dust rang out loud and clear from the back seat. 'Slow down, Rosie. Make sure he sees us this time.'

I'd do more than that, I decided. The poor guy. His bag strap tugged savagely at his shoulder. How far did he have to go? I pulled up and through the open passenger-side window called, 'Hi! Can we give you a lift?'

The back seat went strangely silent. A young man's face dipped low enough to peer through the window. Hey, it wasn't a bad face either. Olive skin, smooth without a single acne scar, every hair in place, even after a whole day at school. Todd Rooney smiled uncertainly at me then looked in the back seat. 'Oh, hi, Justine.'

Someone behind me was laying an egg.

'We're not going anywhere in particular. Can we drop you somewhere?'

'Yeah, OK.' He opened the door and pushed his heavy bag onto the front seat, sliding himself in beside it. Close up, he was even cuter, I must say. This wasn't such a bad idea after all.

Fiona retrieved her voice from wherever it had fled to. 'Great car, eh?'

'A classic,' Todd commented knowledgeably. He turned and smiled at her. Even with my eyes on the road, I could feel the heat from her blushing face.

'How's Mark?' Todd asked Justine, and from the conversation that followed, I worked out the connection between them. Justine's brother Mark played football with Todd and this was how they'd met.

Todd asked me to drop him home, which was just a few streets away, and gave me directions. Turning to speak to the girls in the back seat was a strain, so once we were away from The Grove he turned round and looked straight ahead through the windshield. When he wasn't looking at me, that is.

'Classic car,' he said again.

'It's my grandfather's.'

'Yeah? I've seen it before. Hard to miss a black Mercedes in Prestwidge.' He kept talking, as I kept driving.

This isn't bad, I thought. If driving a black Mercedes leads to encounters like this, I'm going to enjoy the next few months.

Of course, I wasn't the least bit motivated by a desire to beat the A List at their own game. That would be too childish. And if I did sit up a little straighter in my seat, it was only so that I could see the road better, and definitely not to give him my best angle. Oh boy, he noticed, too.

'What's your name?' he asked, as he was thanking me and getting out of the car.

'Rosie Sinclair,' I answered.

'Rosie Sinclair,' he repeated, as though this would help him remember it. I didn't mind if he remembered it at all. No, Todd Rooney, you say it over as many times as you like.

The A List wouldn't speak to me after that. My membership had been short-lived, it seemed. What did I care?

After I had dropped all three girls off at Justine's house, the mobile phone rang again. This time I pressed the Answer button and just listened.

'Larkin?' said a voice after a moment or two.

It wasn't the same man as this morning. Of course it wouldn't be. That guy at least knew that Grandad wouldn't be answering his mobile for a while.

22

'Larkin, is that you? Say something.'

It's not like I was playing a game, teasing the man. The tone of his voice threw me off balance, that's all. I have never heard anything so threatening, and he had done no more than ask for Grandad. But whoever it was lost patience and ended the call.

Grandad's mobile had all the bells and whistles, but as I punched my way through the menu options trying to read the number that had just called it came up blank. Whoever he was, he didn't want to advertise his number over the airwaves. Hardly surprising in Grandad's line of work.

When I got home, I put the mobile in my school bag for safekeeping. But the memory of that voice sent a shiver through my whole body, and for an instant I felt anything but safe.

THREE

PRESTWIDGE IS WHAT THEY USED to call a 'satellite town'. I guess someone in an office block high above the city centre thought up the concept decades ago as a way of keeping the riffraff out of their hair. So surveyors were sent out into the countryside and measured up streets and stuff so they could build little sweat boxes using fibro and tin and a complete lack of imagination. Whole streets have the same house repeated every twenty-five metres. When Prestwidge people visit each other, they never have to ask where the toilet is.

Of course, over the years the buffer zone of open ground between the city and these satellites like

Prestwidge got filled up, so now we are just a huge suburb at the end of the railway line, a splodge on the map about three kilometres across, marked *Battlers, No Hopers and Petty Crooks*.

If you were born in Prestwidge Hospital, they call you a Prestie. I was, and so was Mum, so we belong here. It's not so bad, though to be honest the high school is not the best. One year, every one of our Year Twelves failed the final exams. The newspapers put their class photo on the front page, and there was such a fuss I thought the authorities would all come out and measure our heads or something.

What do they expect, anyway? The place has bog-awful buildings straight off the Cheapest Possible page in the public works catalogue. Some schools have lush turf on their ovals; we've got prickles and dust. Some schools are freshly painted — and I suppose you could say ours is too, while the graffiti is still wet.

No one earns much social status by going to Prestwidge High School, so we Presties have to create our own status symbols. Just now, the absolute *numero uno* of status symbols is the mobile phone.

The trick at first was to have it ring during class. Juvenile, I know, but it was a kind of victory over the demoralised teachers. Justine, Clare and Fiona scored a huge coup the day they arranged for their boyfriends to ring at exactly the same moment. It was impossible to work out where the ringing was coming from and the rings only lasted for three seconds. Just long enough for the rest of us to identify the signature tune of each. The teacher went ape. Not often do I get a smile out of the A List's antics.

This put them in second place on the All-time Great Gotcha List after the legendary Phil Greymouth. A teacher once sent Phil next door to a rowdy classroom once to find out why they were making so much noise. He stuck his head through the door and shouted at them in a voice that could be heard all over the school. 'Shut up, will ya? We're trying to get some sleep in here.'

Smart-arse comments can't be outlawed, but mobile phones can. They must now be turned off during class. School rule. Guess what happened on Wednesday. In the middle of Maths, Grandad's mobile goes off like a burglar alarm. I scrambled pathetically to get at it, throwing everything out of my bag before Mr Tudor's face went from purple to puce.

The kids all thought I was showing off my new toy, along with the Mercedes, and no amount of grovelling to Mr Tudor would change their minds, or his. I stabbed at the buttons and finally turned the damn thing off.

What should I do? Maybe it had been an important message for Paddy. At morning tea, I turned the phone on again. It began to ring sixty seconds later.

'Hello?' I said tentatively.

'Ah, at last. Why did you cut me off before, Paddy?

And for the last hour you've had your phone off the hook, or whatever it is they do with those new things.' The voice was accusing and mildly annoyed, but it certainly wasn't the man who had sent chills up my spine. This was a woman, an old woman by the sound of it, though she had found a bit of juice to tell Paddy off with.

'I'm sorry,' I said politely. 'Paddy's not here.'

The woman hesitated. 'What did you say, Paddy?'

'No, he's not here.' I raised my voice a notch. 'This is his granddaughter speaking.'

'Where is he?' she asked indignantly.

I didn't want to say precisely. 'Er, he's … unavailable.'

The old girl didn't think much of that explanation. 'What do you mean, unavailable? He was supposed to pick me up half an hour ago.'

'I'm sorry, but Paddy won't be picking anyone up for quite a while. He's … um … he's gone away. On holiday.'

'He didn't tell *me*. How will I see my sister?'

Get a bus, I whispered, though not loud enough for the bossy old dear to hear me. I looked at my watch. Three minutes until the bell for the end of morning tea. 'Look, I have to go. Paddy will be back in six months or so. You can call him then. Bye.'

There was something like a squawk down the line and some words as I hit the End button. I could make out a few of them, '… dead by then …', which put me a little on edge. *Who* would be dead by then?

Before I could turn the phone off, it rang again.

'Hello? Hello? Young girl. Are you there? Speak up.'

Young girl! Well, I suppose when you're eighty-something anyone under fifty is a baby. 'Yes, I'm here,' I said.

'Who are you?'

'Rosie Sinclair. Paddy is my grandfather.'

'Is he really going to be away for six months?'

'I'm afraid so. I'm sort of minding his stuff for him. His phone and his car.'

'His car! You've got his car?'

'Yes, but …'

'Oh, that's a relief. Now, I really must get up to visit my sister. Can you come now? I'm already rather late.'

Just then the bell sounded. Kids were moving back to class and I was talking to an old lady who expected me to drive her to her sister's place, *now*!

'I'm sorry,' I said firmly. 'I'm tied up just at present.'

'Well, what time can I expect you?'

Mr Hoskins, the Deputy Principal, appeared in the yard. If he saw me with my ear to a mobile, he would give me a detention for sure. I moved into the hall and headed for my next class. 'I can't come at all.'

'Of course you can, dear. You've got Paddy's Mercedes, haven't you?'

'Yes, but …'

She cut me off again. 'Will it be this morning?'

28

Mr Tudor saw me from inside his classroom. I had to end this call NOW.

I've never been good under pressure. 'I can't get away until after three,' I said.

'Good. I'll expect you after three, then.'

That was that. End. I was inside the classroom before I realised that I didn't have a clue who I'd been talking to, let alone where she lived. In a way, this was a sort of revenge against the old darling who had left me so flustered.

At lunch time the phone rang again. 'You don't know who I am or where I live.'

'Sorry,' I said meekly.

'Mrs Foat.' She gave me the address. 'After three, then. I've let them know I'm coming.'

Grandad had asked me to do a few errands, so I suppose it was only fair, like payment for having the car. After school I refused all pleas for a lift and headed off to the address Mrs Foat had given me, using the street directory from the glove box.

She seemed a frail old thing, but I wasn't fooled. I'd seen her at work, or heard her from the wrong end of the line, anyway. Of course, now she was as gracious as the Queen of England. 'So good of you,' she purred, when I helped her down the steps. How does she get up and down this staircase by herself? I wondered.

The sister's name was Meredith, and she wasn't in a house of her own like Mrs Foat. She was in hospital. Poor dear. Her wasted body was still there in the bed, but her mind had left the building. Paddy Larkin wouldn't be out in time for *this* funeral. I could work that much out.

Mrs Foat told me she would be ready to go home at five. That meant I was free until then, I supposed. Thanks a lot. I'll go have a smoke and polish the limo. Maybe I *would* be needing a chauffeur's cap.

Then at five it was back to Mrs Foat's house. There didn't seem to be a Mr Foat any more, though there was evidence that a man had lived here once. The handyman repair to the back door that wasn't quite right, the dusty tools on a work bench that I could see in a room that ran off the kitchen. The photos gave the game away. She saw me looking at them. 'He's been gone ten years. If it wasn't for those, I'm afraid I would have forgotten his face.' She said all of this in a matter-of-fact tone, without a glance in my direction. She was a shrewd old thing, as I had already learned, and she guessed what I was thinking. 'That sounds terrible to you, I suppose.'

Well, it did, to tell you the truth, but of course I didn't say so to her. What's love if you can't remember your husband's face? But she had moved on without looking at me.

'Here,' she said, holding out her hand.

I opened my palm and into it dropped a two-dollar coin. 'What's this for?'

'The ride, of course. I always pay Paddy.'

Two bucks. Great! No wonder he turned to crime.

But I thanked her, didn't I, and went home to find out which diet fad Mum was into this week. Just my luck. Eggplant and Lemon Juice, or something like that. I hate eggplant. Why doesn't someone come up with the Hamburger and Chocolate Diet? Honestly, people have no imagination.

FOUR

At morning tea on Thursday, I sat with the phone in my hands. To switch on or not to switch on? That was the question. If this sounds like a familiar line it's because we'd been doing *Hamlet* for two periods straight.

> *Whether 'tis nobler in the mind to suffer*
> *The demanding phone calls of outrageous*
> * old folk*
> *Or to turn my back on their sea of troubles*
> *And by ignoring them, get a life.*

Sorry, Mr Shakespeare.

I already had one gig for the afternoon. A Mrs Giastacomo had rung before I left for school. Her husband needed to go to the doctor and she wanted to know what time to make the appointment for. Not *Please could they get a ride in the black taxi?* Just *When*!

I told her four o'clock.

Why should I spend all afternoon running errands for my grandfather's friends? I had assignments and stuff.

Oh, all right. I had assignments, but I was more likely to spend my time doing *stuff*.

I do have friends, though to be honest they mostly have jobs that don't finish until five p.m., and my best friend Glenda goes to uni and often has late lectures. (More on her later.) But hey, I've got the keys to a fantastic car. I could just go cruising, maybe pick up that friend of the A List girls on his way home from the station. All sorts of possibilities. Bugger them. I'm not a granny nanny.

Then I had a flash of yesterday with Mrs Foat. There was no bus route near her place. She couldn't go to see her sister unless someone took her. The stairs in and out of her house were dangerous. And two dollars! A cab would cost fifteen, in each direction. Thirty dollars was probably more than she spent on food for a week. What if she starved, just so she could afford to go and visit her sister? She'd end up next to her in the cemetery before Paddy ever saw her again.

So I turned on the phone. It rang two minutes later.

'Oh, there you are, Paddy. I've been trying for hours.'

It was a man this time. An old man. I told him the drill. He told me what he needed. His name was Eric Duval. Paddy took Mr and Mrs Duval down to the shops each week. Late afternoon was fine. I told him four-thirty.

Bloody conscience.

The Giastacomos' place was falling down around them. When I went inside I found out why. Mrs G was in a wheelchair. She could get around the house pretty well, and because things had been altered to make it easier for her she could get in and out of bed on her own and even cook meals. But Mr G wasn't much use. He was still steady on his pins, but it was in the marble department that he had trouble. Most of them had rolled out of the ring. Mrs Giastacomo saw the look on my face when I met him. 'He's got Alzheimer's, dear. That's why he needs another visit to the doctor.'

'Shouldn't you two have a nurse or something?' I asked without thinking.

I was ready to bawl my eyes out by the time she had explained. If they had asked me to cook and clean for them, do the shopping and rock them to sleep for the rest of their lives, I'm sure I would have agreed. Fortunately, Mr G just needed a lift to the doctor's surgery.

'Where are we going?' asked Mr G when I managed to get him into the back seat of the Mercedes. He didn't recognise the surgery when we arrived, but he seemed to react well when the receptionist greeted him kindly.

He looked straight at me and said, 'Thank you, Amelia. Where are the children?' He looked around the waiting room at the other patients as though someone were trying to fob the wrong grandchildren off on him.

The receptionist filled me in. 'Amelia is his daughter. She used to drive him around the place in a car full of screaming kids, but she's moved away now. He's got two sons somewhere but neither of them lifts a finger to help him. Thanks for bringing him in. He'll be ready to go home in an hour.'

I was running late for the Duvals. I gunned the Merc — nice feeling. All that power under my foot. I was starting to understand what the petrol-heads get so excited about.

The Duvals had no problems in the marble department. In fact, they were absolutely charming in the old-fashioned way. They offered me a cup of tea before we started and asked about Paddy in a sensitive way that told me, without actually using the word, that they had found out he was in prison.

'Isn't she a pretty girl, Eric?' exclaimed Mrs Duval, who told me to call her Janice.

'Pretty? Why, she's beautiful!' he answered, topping her.

Mrs Duval knew she had been trumped. She simply smiled and won me over with a chocolate biscuit. They made sure the last two chocolate biscuits were only eaten on the day they went shopping for more. It was Mrs Duval's biscuit that I was offered. The pair of them were quietly competing for my favour. What a wonderful old couple, I thought to myself, which I suppose sounds a bit condescending.

During the drive to the supermarket we explored my place in the Larkin family tree. They knew more about my family than I did. I was so taken with their sweet and gentle ways that I joined them inside to push the trolley around. Maybe I was being manipulated by their charm, but they had it all over Mrs Foat in that department.

Then, who did I spot but Todd Rooney. He had already seen me. Waved. He was coming my way. We exchanged hellos and then he held back. He thinks these two are my grandparents, I realised. 'Just doing an errand,' I said, worried how this would sound to the Duvals, but luckily they had moved out of earshot.

'Me too. Getting a few things for Mum,' Todd said, holding up a basket with the leafy end of some celery poking over the end. A lot of guys would worry they looked unmanly carrying a basket like that, but he didn't seem to mind and he certainly didn't look unmanly from where I was standing. I wondered what the skin of his chin would feel like if I ran my finger lightly along ...

Oh, sorry. Just daydreaming. I still had the trolley and the Duvals were waiting patiently for me at the end of the aisle. 'Do you need a lift home?' I asked Todd.

'Wouldn't mind.'

Neither would I.

Todd had everything he needed already, so he sauntered along beside me as I followed the Duvals. Don't ask me what we talked about. It was one of those nothing conversations where the fact that you were walking side by side was more important than anything that you said.

'Don't forget the cinnamon, Janice,' said Mr Duval. 'You know you don't enjoy your bingo without a bit of cinnamon cake.'

How cute can you get? Grandad was partial to a bit of cinnamon cake as well, I remembered. Must be an oldies thing.

We took the lift down to the car park where I had left the Mercedes, but as soon as I opened the front door I had the strangest feeling. I smelled smoke — not the smoke of an engine fire or burning upholstery, thank God, but cigarette smoke. Since I was trying to quit and on Grandad's orders I hadn't let anyone else smoke in the car, this set alarm bells ringing in my head.

The Duvals didn't notice anything, and neither did Todd. There was no reason why they should. But that whiff of stale smoke made me suspect someone had been in the car. I looked around, but there wasn't anything in the car to steal except maybe the street directory in the glove box. Who would bother? If someone wanted to break in, surely it would be to steal the car itself. And how would they do it without leaving any trace?

You're imagining things, I told myself. Maybe the tobacco smell is on Todd's breath and you just haven't noticed it before. Everything seemed in its place in the glove box, as far as I could tell.

'What's wrong?' Todd asked me, when he found me leaning awkwardly across him to explore it. (Not that I felt the slightest bit awkward leaning across his body.)

I settled back into the driver's seat. 'Oh, nothing,' I assured him, and by the time we had left the car park I'd put that unsettled feeling out of my mind.

With the Duvals in the back seat, there wasn't much chance to talk to Todd. He seemed intimidated by their presence and kept looking back over his shoulder. Hmm, I thought. What am I missing out on here? And for the first time, I felt a touch of irritation towards the elderly couple.

When I pulled up outside his house, Todd asked me where I lived.

'Oh, way over on the other side of the high school. Not far in the car, though.'

'No, I mean what street?'

I told him and he seemed relieved. The smile he gave as he said thanks hit me like a camera flash. Oh, boy!

The Duvals saw it too. They had watched and listened intently every inch of the way to Todd's. 'What a handsome boy,' Mrs Duval said as soon as I'd pulled away from the curb. 'And nice, too. A real charmer.'

There was no missing what she was getting at, but it was Mr Duval who stunned me. 'You know why he wanted to know what street you live in, don't you, Rosie?'

I acted dumb. Actually, I *was* dumb! Mr Duval had to fill me in. 'If you know a girl's name and where she lives, you can find her number in the phone book, can't you? Worked that one out for myself when I was a lot younger!'

They had phones back in the time of the dinosaurs? I looked in the rear-view mirror. The pair of them were smiling at me, that gentle, friendly smile that had already won me over.

And I tell you what, Mr Duval was right, but it was an hour or two before I found out. In the meantime, it was back to the doctor's surgery for Mr Giastacomo.

'Who are you?' he asked me, but he went with me anyway. I suppose when you're eighty-something, you're not worried about being kidnapped.

Mrs G was very thankful. She gave me a dollar. Add that to the two dollars the Duvals had pressed into my hand and I was well on my way to a life of luxury.

Feeling the coins jingle together in my pocket made me laugh. I slipped in behind the wheel of Paddy Larkin's black taxi. This wasn't half bad, you know. Yep, I felt great. A regular Mother Teresa.

Things got even better. Todd called just before six. 'I hope you don't mind. I found your number in the phone book.'

Right first time, Eric Duval!

'Would you like to go to a party on Saturday night?'

I certainly *would* like to go to a party, particularly if it meant going with Todd Rooney! Justine, eat your heart out! The A List would go ballistic if word got around that I was going out with Todd. Did I say 'if'? It was more a matter of 'when' — and if the rumours were slow in starting, I could always nudge them along myself.

Then at ten-thirty, when I was thinking about bed, the mobile rang. Some old codger's up late, I thought. I hope I don't have to drive him to the hospital at this hour.

'Hello?'

'Where's Larkin? Tell him I want to speak to him.' It was that awful ice-hard voice from two days ago.

'Grandad's not here. You can't talk to him.' Then, like an idiot, I asked if I could take a message.

'Message!' says the voice. 'Yeah, you tell him this. I want the ring.'

'What ring?'

'He knows. Tell him I know he's got it and he'd better cough it up.'

'I don't understand ...' I started to say, but by then I was talking to myself.

FIVE

On Friday the mobile stayed silent right through morning recess and lunch time as well. Maybe old people are too tired to go anywhere by the end of the week. When you're old, even doing next to nothing all week can get tiring. As for the guy who wanted that ring from Grandad ... no news was good news.

I went to see Glenda after school. She's always home from uni by three on a Friday to get ready for her night job. (More of that in a minute.) Glenda is my closest friend, and because we talk every few days on the phone, she already knew about the Mercedes. When I pulled up she came out to kick the tyres anyway. 'Has he got a BMW he wants minded? Tell him I'm available.'

Glenda had had her education retarded by Prestwidge High School the same way as me, but considering she was two years ahead (and two years older) it's a miracle that we ever got together at all. My mother's hairdressing salon was the connection. I wasn't enjoying school by the end of Year Ten, so when Mum suggested I pack it in and become her apprentice I jumped at the chance. She's always considered too much education to be dangerous for a girl. 'Like putting a V8 engine in a cute little sports car,' she said once. I think Mum's got a four-cylinder under the bonnet, if you get my meaning.

At the time I finished Year Ten, Glenda had just finished Year Twelve, and because she desperately needed the money to get away from her booze-sozzled father, she started up as the other apprentice and promptly moved out of home. We hit it off straightaway, and just as well, too, because we both quickly discovered that we hated hair and heads and the smell of perming fluid.

The truth really hit home whenever we looked over at Tracey. She's been working for Mum for twenty years now. It's not that she's not a nice person or anything. She's quite good looking for a forty-something, wears tight little skirts that get the guys looking in the window, I've noticed. Despite having access to whatever hair colour she likes, she's stayed a fine auburn for as long as I've known her.

She's very like Mum, which I suppose is why they get on so well together, and that was just it. Glenda and I looked at each other and realised that this was our life, as good as it was going to get if we worked out our apprenticeships. We didn't want to be just two more Traceys in a world already full of them.

But we were stuck with the job for the whole of that long, long year — Glenda because she needed the money and me because my mother wouldn't let me mooch around doing nothing. (She already had a son doing that, after all.)

The thing about Glenda, though, is her ambition. She doesn't want to stay a Prestie all her life, and after a year working with the outside of people's heads, she announced that she wanted to work with the inside. She enrolled to study Psychology at uni, starting the next year, and to everyone's surprise but her own, she was accepted.

The trouble was she wanted to go to uni full-time, and that meant she couldn't hold down a day job. That's where this story gets a bit ... well ... exotic. Literally. To pay the bills, Glenda started up as an exotic dancer at a club in the city. Now, everybody knows that 'exotic dancer' is code for something a bit more basic, so I should point out that Glenda has the sort of body that men undress with their eyes when she walks around The Grove. All that's changed is that these days she gets paid to let them see what they spend so much time imagining. Makes sense to me. Some people would be disgusted, I suppose, but Glenda's motto is 'What you see is all you get.' Her stage name is 'Giselle'. Go, Giselle!

As for Rosie Sinclair, I found all this thoroughly inspiring (except for the stripping part), so I went back to finish Year Eleven and Twelve. There wasn't much else to do anyway, and no-one to do it with. The only Prestie girls who weren't in classrooms pushed a pram in front of them wherever they went, and I wasn't going there, thanks very much. Anyway, school isn't so bad now. I won an academic award last semester. Third in Maths. Mum liked the idea of my scoring good marks occasionally, but in Maths! I made a big show of shaving my legs just to reassure her.

'I've met a boy,' I told Glenda once she'd stopped staring at the car. 'His name's Todd. He's asked me to a party on Saturday night.'

'Good-looking?'

'Gorgeous. And a bit shy, too. He's so cute, I could wrap him up and take him home.'

Glenda always cut straight to the important issues. 'What will you wear?'

Oh, God ... and things had been going so well. I looked in the mirror. Long black hair to my shoulders, little chocolate circles in the middle of my eyes, nice legs, a bust line that made boys look. I liked what I saw, even the little freckles on my nose. It was what I *couldn't* see that was the problem. I carry all my worries behind me — in my bottom, in other words. It's enormous. I could sell advertising space. There are islands in the Pacific Ocean smaller than my bum.

'Stop stressing about your bum,' scolded Glenda.

'I can't help it.'

'It's magnificent.'

'Magnificently huge. That's the problem.'

'Look, we've been over this a hundred times and I'm sick of it,' she said with a genuine hint of warning in her voice. 'You have the perfect backside. It's round, it's there, enjoy it.'

'Maybe I could get one side amputated and have the rest sort of spread out.'

'It's not like peanut butter you can shove around on a piece of toast.' Glenda gave me her exasperated look, so I backed off. Maybe I'd put her through all this just so she would say nice things about my bum. It can be a bit soul-destroying when you hang around with someone with a perfect figure. (It didn't help that Glenda/Giselle was getting her amazing outfits ready as we spoke, holding up each skimpy little piece in front of her then stuffing it into her carry bag or discarding it on the bed beside me.) 'The only butt you should worry about is this boy's,' she reminded me.

'It looks pretty good to me, I must admit. What I've seen of it through his school uniform, anyway.'

She smiled. 'It makes a change to be discussing *your* love life instead of *mine*.'

That was the downside of being Giselle. Glenda had guys asking her out all the time, but they were all creeps. I kept hoping she would find someone nice. Maybe I had beaten her to it.

At least I could be sure she wouldn't steal Todd away from me, no matter how good-looking she was. That was the advantage of having a girlfriend two years older. All the guys my age were too immature for her. Mind you, I had my own problems in that regard. The guys at school seemed so much younger than me. Little boys, really. All they talked about was football and beer and cars. Mum tells me they never grow out of this, that even as grown men, their only topics of conversation will be football and beer and cars. She says I should count myself lucky they talk at all instead of just grunting like baboons. I'm hoping she's got it wrong. (It wouldn't be the first time.) But come to think of it, boys don't say much at all around me. I can't understand why.

'How's it going with the geriatrics?' Glenda asked, to change the subject. I'd had a whinge to her on the phone about my 'errands' last night. 'None today.'

I hadn't told her about the two calls from that cold and sinister voice, or the smell of cigarette smoke in the Mercedes. I did now, as matter-of-factly as I could, because to be honest, it all had me a little rattled. How could a guy cram so much menace into a few simple words? And why would anyone break into the Merc?

'Your grandad's car? That's serious.'

'I'm not sure about the car. Could be my imagination.'

'But not the phone calls,' said Glenda as she fixed me with a concerned eye. 'Do you know what ring he's talking about?'

'No, Grandad's not into jewellery. He doesn't even wear a wedding ring, and Grandma's fingers aren't exactly dripping with diamonds. Just her engagement ring. Nothing else. He wouldn't touch stolen jewellery. He reckons it's too hard to know what's real and what's fake.'

'Well, someone thinks he's made an exception,' Glenda commented. She picked up her bag. 'Hey, could you drive me into the club? I can arrive in style for once. Should make the bouncers out front sit up and take notice.'

SIX

SATURDAY WAS THE EARLIEST WE were allowed to visit Grandad in what they called the 'correctional facility'. Seriously creepy. High fences, razor wire, watchtowers. If Mum hadn't been crying already, this alone would have been enough to set her off. And Grandma is a tough old bird in her own way, but I saw the blood drain out of her face as we drove into the car park. There wasn't much left in mine either, I can tell you.

Paddy acted as upbeat as he could manage, to save the feelings of 'his girls', but I could see being in this place was no picnic. You would think the Mercedes would be well down the list of things to talk about, but there were lots of awkward silences that day and one of us would have to jump in with a new direction for the conversation just to get the words moving again.

'Have you had any calls on my mobile, Rosie?' Grandad asked.

Any! Better to ask how many. I listed them off: Mrs Foat, the Giastacomos, the Duvals and a few others I had managed to squeeze in between sleeping, eating and going to school. He smiled widely. If this was what it took to raise his spirits, then maybe all those errands had been worth it.

'They just need a little help getting around, Rosie,' he said. 'Fiercely independent people, you understand. I really appreciate it, and so do they, even if they would never admit how much they need that car of mine. You made them pay, didn't you?'

'What! A dollar or two each. Yeah, I'll have enough to buy my own block of chocolate soon.' Actually, that was just a slip of the tongue. It's not like I would ever buy a whole block of chocolate just for myself (though if I did, it would be the type with bright green mint inside). No, chocolate goes straight to my problem area, if you know what I mean.

Thinking about chocolate distracted me for a moment, but I could see what was going on. Grandad was manipulating me, of course. He knew I would do anything for him and he had already guessed that I was a sucker for his bunch of equally manipulative eighty-year-olds. The more he beamed, the more I felt obliged to keep it up.

'Look, about the petrol. I've got an account at Ferguson's garage on Pine Street. Fergo knows the car. He owes me a few favours. Just tell him who you are and he'll fill it up for you as often as you need.' He winked at me devilishly and I began to wonder whether every oil filter and spark plug at that particular garage had made its way there illegally.

Time was up. Hugs all round, a Niagara of tears, many of them mine.

I still hadn't been able to ask Grandad about the ring. How could I get a few seconds alone with him? To my surprise, he seemed as keen to have a private word as I was. Then Mum ushered Grandma off towards the door and suddenly we had the moment we needed.

'Rosie! Rosie!' he whispered urgently. 'You've met the Duvals, haven't you?'

I grinned. 'Yes. They're so sweet. I took them shopping.'

'Shopping. That was all, was it?' The grin dropped from my face. He seemed rather agitated and eager to tell me something. 'Look, I should have warned you about those two. It's the French blood, if you ask me.'

French blood? What was he talking about? Mum turned at the door, looking as though she was about to charge back to Grandad and strangle him in another desperate bear hug. If I didn't ask my question now, I would miss my chance.

'Grandad, there was a call on your mobile. The guy didn't give his name, but his voice was … well, it was sort of threatening. He said he wants the ring back.'

'What ring?'

My heart sank. It wasn't just his words or the tone of his voice. Even the look on his face told me he didn't have a clue what I was talking about.

Then the guard was there, telling Grandad sternly that it was time to go back through the heavily barred door. Paddy's last words showed that he had forgotten about my question already. He was back to what seemed to matter most to him. 'The Duvals, Rosie. Just be discreet, OK.'

Discreet. He had me worried now. Were they into shoplifting? Should I search their cardigans before we went through the checkout?

I didn't have time to think any more about it. Mum and I had to get Grandma back to the car. She hadn't cried much, but she seemed about to have one of her fainting fits all the same. Just as well I had been getting lots of practice guiding old people around by the arm. Grandma wasn't so old, really, but she sure seemed that way on our walk back to the Mercedes.

When we arrived back at our place, Uncle Bruce was there. Slimeball. I wondered how he had made his way over here without a car or a friend to drive him. His wet clothes told the story. It had rained all morning, and Bruce's jacket was just damp enough to show he had been out in it for a few minutes here and there. Public transport. He must have caught the bus and walked from the stop two blocks away. How the mighty had fallen.

'Did you enjoy the bus ride?' I asked him maliciously.

He gave me a filthy look. It was all I could do to stifle a loud laugh. Absolute bitch, eh? I made a show of locking the Mercedes and slipping the key into my pocket.

'You should have come to the prison with us,' chastised Grandma.

Ha! Bruce was afraid they would keep him there, where he belongs. I fantasised about him behind bars. Mmm. Warm, happy feeling. It's not like he cares about his own father in the slightest — I'm sure he only turned up at court to make sure Grandad didn't incriminate him.

'What are you doing here, anyway?' I asked him bluntly.

His narrow eyes opened wide. He'd been caught out. 'Came to see you,' he told Grandma. I guessed he was actually here to see Mum, and that normally meant he needed money.

Even Mum had worked this out, because she was already glancing towards her handbag with a long face. Hair by Sinclair would never make us rich, but it paid the bills, due entirely to the fact that all the woman in Prestwidge *did* want to look the same and went to my mother to make sure of it. 'How much do you need, Bruce?' she asked, resigning herself to the inevitable.

'Cynthia,' he chided, his arms wide. 'I haven't come looking for money.'

Mum's face brightened for an instant, then the light went out. If he didn't want money, what *did* he want?

I made the tea and we sat around the kitchen table discussing Grandad. They were on to the second pot when I noticed that Bruce had gone missing. He obviously had a low sympathy threshold. I'd like to test his *pain* threshold, though.

If he wasn't in the kitchen, where had he gone? I checked the lounge room, expecting to find him in front of the TV with Jason. Nope, Jason hadn't seen him, and there was no-one in the bathroom either. He must be outside. My steps quickened then, because the only thing outside likely to interest Uncle Bruce was the Mercedes.

I was just in time. He had managed to break in without any trouble, and there he was, on his hands and knees inside the car, not the faintest trace of guilt on his face. 'You're keeping it nice, Rosie,' he commented. 'Very clean.'

'Grandad left it with *me*, remember? You haven't even got a licence at the moment,' I added cruelly.

He didn't seem hurt, and in fact he barely even looked up at me. 'Of course, of course,' he muttered as he crawled along the seat towards the far door. 'I wouldn't *think* of borrowing it without asking you.' He had climbed out on the opposite side by this time and wandered back towards the house.

I locked the car again and put the key in the pocket of my jeans as I followed. What could I have done if he had got it started and driven off? I was hardly going to call the police when the first thing they would do was impound the Mercedes.

But there was another matter that niggled at me as I returned to the house. He had been in the back seat, not the driver's seat. Since when did car thieves hot-wire the ignition from the back seat? There was something very odd going on here.

SEVEN

Meet the Eisenberg sisters.

Appearance: pretty much identical. Tall and downright skinny — though to my eyes anyone with a butt that doesn't hang over the edge of her seat is skinny. (Bloody problem area!) Both have shortish, schoolteacher hair, all of it grey.

Clothing: 1950s 'Prestwidge Chic', which is what my English teacher would call an oxymoron. (Look it up!) Pleated skirts aplenty teamed with sensible shoes, the kind with hard heels that make a satisfying rap on the pavement when the sisters get into one of their lock-step walks.

Marital status: single. There was a suggestion that

Caroline had a fiancé once, and of course there were the rumours about the Anglican priest, but neither has ever actually married.

Living arrangements: the Eisenberg sisters were born into a wealthy family in the leafy suburbs close to the city. However, the family fell on hard times, and these days the sisters live in a modest little house in Prestwidge. (Fell on hard times! That's about as far as anyone can fall and still remain on planet Earth.)

Age: no, they are not twins. Everyone thinks they are, because they look so much alike, but Deirdre is eighty-four and Caroline a mere filly by comparison, at eighty-two.

Favourite pastime: debating. (That's a euphemism. Go look it up too!)

I knew all this about the Eisenberg sisters after my year at Hair by Sinclair. Their mother was a world champion gossip, according to Mum — and it takes one to know one. If these sisters are now in their eighties, it is no surprise that their mother passed over long ago to that great sewing circle in the sky, but not before she developed the ultimate system for tattletales.

Apparently, she would pore over the Births and Marriages section of the newspaper and keep her own register of dates. With a calendar, a bit of simple subtraction and the knowledge that it takes nine months to brew up a baby, she was able to discover which young brides had already been up the duff when they walked down the aisle. This wouldn't have given her much clout in Prestwidge, where half the mothers have never been near a church. But it mattered in the high society of the inner city — and we're talking a long time ago, too, when there were still such things as Public Morals. Old Mrs Eisenberg was their foremost defender.

That was, until a new Anglican priest arrived. He was young(ish), drop-dead handsome and convinced of a new way to God, or something like that. He told Mrs Eisenberg that her crusade against immorality did not sit comfortably with the modern vision of a loving and accepting God. He suggested to her that young girls who found themselves 'in trouble' might actually need the community's help rather than their scorn.

Mrs Eisenberg had a stroke.

Young Father Windshuttle was a great comfort to the sisters during the weeks it took for their ghastly mother to breathe her last poisonous breath. By then, gossip of a new kind had surrounded the sisters. Their infatuation with the young priest was obvious in their moistened eyes, and because he was only two years younger than Caroline, and certainly not out of the question for Deirdre either, speculation was rife that both sisters kindled a secret flame. Maybe they did, but Father Windshuttle was careful he didn't get burned. Instead he married the bishop's daughter and ended up Dean of the Cathedral.

Even more unfortunately for the Eisenberg sisters, their mother in her wisdom had considered that mere thirty-somethings couldn't manage their own finances. In the terms of her will, an uncle, who was all tweed suits and stupidity, took control of their money. He lost most of the dough on dodgy business ventures in New Guinea and then drank the rest. The family home was sold to pay the debts he had racked up, and by the time they laid the old reprobate to rest beside his sister, there was barely enough left to buy a hovel in the brand-new town of Prestwidge.

You've got to admire the sisters, though. They didn't become bitter. Inspired by Reverend Windshuttle, they turned their talents and energy to good works. They became members of every committee in every organisation from the church to the RSL, and then in retirement they founded the XYZ Club. (Stands for Xtra Years of Zest — it's a thing for wrinklies, to keep them chirping happily until they fall off the perch.)

That was where they wanted me to take them when Caroline rang early on Saturday morning, an XYZ function. I flicked the Merc into life and went to pick them up.

Now, I know my way around Prestwidge a bit, certainly round The Grove and anywhere else where you are likely to find (a) decent clothes or (b) decent guys. Other areas can be a mystery, I admit.

'Did Paddy tell you where to go, Rosie?' one of the sisters asked. I think it was Deirdre, though I was still learning which was which.

'No, I haven't spoken to Grandad at all, really.'

'We'll direct you, then.'

Famous last words.

The one I thought must be Deirdre jumped in first, since she had asked the question. 'You get onto Maplethorpe Road, as though you're going to Martindale ...'

Caroline cut her off. 'Heavens, no. The poor girl doesn't want to be bothered with main roads at this time of day. Rosie, if you'll just take us to the end of the street and turn left.'

I turned round in the seat and reached for the key in the ignition, but before I could start the engine, Deirdre made her counterattack. 'No, not left. We'll get caught at the lights. They take forever to change at that intersection.'

The contradictions continued. First I was to go one way, then the other would disagree. Anyone else I know who set to like this would have been shouting at each other before long, but not these two. Everything was said in the politest of gentle voices. But we were going nowhere. I couldn't make a start until they had made up their minds.

Three minutes, four. Then it occurred to me. They weren't *going* to make up their minds. They were having too much fun, by the look of things.

'What's the actual address?' I asked from the front seat.

'Fifty-nine Timson Street,' said Caroline.

'Fifty-three,' corrected Deirdre.

It didn't matter. I had them now. I took Paddy's street directory out of the glove box and looked up Timson Street. Easy-peasy. Once I had turned the first corner, the sisters stopped debating the best route and sat back to enjoy the ride. It wasn't very far in the end, and before I knew it I was heading home again, my mind already grappling with the crucial question of what to wear on my date tonight with Todd.

Of course, this took up a lot of my concentration and didn't leave a lot for driving, but what happened next still wasn't my fault. It was the silver Commodore that cut sharply in front of *me*. I mean, you can't blame *me* for someone else's bad manners. No warning, no indicator light. It was almost like he was *trying* to force me into the gutter. Bloody lunatic. I wished I'd had time to catch his number plate, because I would have put the cops onto him, even if I am Paddy Larkin's granddaughter.

It was more luck than good driving that avoided a collision. How could I have explained that to poor Grandad? And I bet the mongrel driving that silver Commodore wouldn't have stopped if he had put a dent in the Mercedes either, because he took off like bat out of hell straight afterwards.

The whole incident left me a little shaken, I must admit.

But the Mercedes didn't miss a beat, as though close shaves like that were just part of life. Oh, great! Now I'm taking life lessons from a car!

Glenda never gets out of bed before two on a Saturday, which is hardly surprising when you remember that Giselle only finishes work at five a.m. I waited until two-thirty then went round, the back seat of the Mercedes covered with the five different outfits I was trying to choose between for the big date.

'Skirt or pants, d'you reckon?'

'You've got great legs, Rosie. Show them off.'

A skirt, then. But *which* skirt? Glenda didn't like any of the ones I'd brought with me.

'You want to knock his eyeballs out, don't you?' She pulled out one of her own. (I've explained about Glenda's figure, haven't I?) I squeezed inside it, but only just. It was black, made of shiny fake leather and very, very short.

'What does it look like from behind?'

'Will you stop obsessing about your bum!' She stood back for the view that I couldn't get of myself. 'Fantastic,' she said. 'His brains will fry the minute he sees you.'

She inspected the tops I'd brought with me. 'This one.' It was a simple pale pink affair, and also rather tight in the best places. The view in the mirror wasn't half bad, especially of my legs, which I'm rather proud of. But that skirt ... 'I look a bit tarty, don't you think?'

'I'm not the one to ask. Come on. Be daring.' It was her favourite line.

I caught a little of her resolve. 'OK,' I said uncertainly.

My resolve lasted three hours, until I had to dress for the real thing. The pink top was cute, but that skirt was too much for a first date. I put on my own little black skirt. *Much* better.

We had agreed that I would drive. Todd saw me pull up outside his house and came out onto the footpath to meet me. But instead of jumping in straightaway, he leaned through the window and invited me inside.

There was his mother, smiling warmly. She had the air of a nurse about her, a bad case of hat hair, flat shoes and a mouth that didn't have to speak to tell you what she thought of you. Thank God I'd switched outfits. Mr Rooney came in from the kitchen and checked out my pink top. (Hello! Hello! My face is up here! That's better.) I won a smile from him, too — a bit different from the one his wife had given me. Then it was goodbye to the parents and back to the car.

'Rosie, do you mind if we pick up some friends of mine along the way?' Todd asked suddenly, after we had driven three blocks.

Alarms bells went off inside my head. 'Yeah, OK,' I agreed reluctantly.

There were three friends, it seemed. Two guys from Todd's school and a girl named Alicia. The boys were weighed down by a six-pack of stubbies in each hand. Alicia was weighed down by a tonne of mascara. It set off her bleached blonde hair nicely. If she was aiming for the slutty look she had hit the bullseye.

The party was being held by one of Todd's private school mates who lived well beyond Prestie territory.

It was a twenty-minute drive, and in that time Todd tried three or four times to get me talking. I kept my eyes firmly on the road and my mouth pretty well clamped. Inside my head, though, the language was flying. *The rotten mongrel. He's just using me to get himself and his friends to a party. I'm nothing but a stupid taxi driver to him.*

When we arrived he let the others go ahead then looked me in the face. 'Hey, listen, I'm sorry about that lot. They couldn't get here any other way, so I kind of conned you a bit, but it's you I really want to be with.' He took my hand and gave it a gentle squeeze, and along with that lightbulb smile, it thawed me out a little. 'Do you want a drink?'

'I'm driving.'

He came back with a Coke and a beer and told me how great I looked. The charm offensive was in full swing, and to be honest, it was working. He introduced me to a few people and I could see the envy in the girls' eyes. Soon I was laughing along with the rest of them.

There was a live band out in the back yard, and when they started up Todd asked me to dance. Now, as it happens, I like dancing even more than eating chocolate (not that I *ever* do that!), so he didn't have to ask twice. The band was great, but the real surprise was Todd. So many guys are self-conscious when they dance, making pathetic little movements with their hips and hands that show they really just want the set to finish so they can get back to drinking. Not Todd

Rooney. He was jumping like a demented Masai warrior — one with impeccable rhythm.

The real surprise came during the break between sets. 'Hey, Rosie, come and meet the band,' he says, dragging me along by the hand. They greeted him like a soul brother and I soon discovered that they were all his classmates too, a garage band out on their first gig.

Next thing I know, Todd has the drumsticks in his hand and he's settling in to drum the next set. He was fantastic. I danced in front of the bass drum, feeling the vibration hit me like a bomb and waving away any guys who wanted to dance with me. Try dancing next to a whole drum kit some time. It's awesome.

By the time the police arrived, I'd lost the feeling in my legs. Alicia, meanwhile, was off her face, and Todd's two mates weren't much better. The cops decided that since it was already after midnight everyone should go home. We managed to get all three of our passengers into the car, but Alicia really didn't look well. Every time she lay back in the seat she complained that she felt sick, but when she tried to sit upright her head flopped around like a sleeping baby's. A kilometre from her place, it finally didn't matter whether she was sitting up or lying back. 'I'm going be sick,' she announced.

'Not in this car, you're not,' I said rather heartlessly. I managed to pull over without causing a major accident. Just in time, too, because Alicia let rip like Mount Vesuvius before we could even get her out of the car. The boys copped a good deal of it. 'Oh shit. That's disgusting,' one wailed. But we could barely hear him above the moaning of dearest Alicia.

I opened the door, dreading the scene I'd find behind me, but Todd was out of his seat already, helping Alicia onto the grassy footpath. He held her shoulders while she was spectacularly sick again, then cleaned her up and his mates too. They were lucky he was there. I'd been ready to drive off. We dumped them at home eventually, and thanks to Todd, their stink went with them. I drove to his place.

So.

There we were.

Parked.

Outside Todd's house.

All the lights were out except for one over the front porch. Nice touch. We did the small talk thing about what a great night it had been.

Things went quiet.

He thanked me for doing all the driving.

Things went quiet again.

Then he kissed me. Once. A sort of smooch that lasted about three seconds flat, and before I knew it he was on the footpath, smiling that electric smile. Like a robot, I started the engine and moved forward so he could wave me off to the end of the street.

And that was that!

EIGHT

'NOW LET ME GET THIS straight,' said Glenda. 'He kissed you good night but you can't make up your mind whether you are pleased or disappointed.'

She was sitting on the kitchen bench, a bowl of cereal balanced in one hand, a spoon in the other, even though it was three o'clock on Sunday afternoon. (Giselle worked Saturday nights as well.)

I nodded uncertainly in answer to her question.

'OK, so let's review the facts.' This was another of her favourite sayings. She put down the bowl and the spoon and started to count off the evidence on her fingers.

'Fact one: he's gorgeous.'

I nodded.

'Fact two: he's fun to be with. Three: you had a great time. Four: he's a great dancer.'

She had four fingers poking out from her palm now. I shrugged a shoulder and sniffed. 'Yes, yes and yes.'

'He plays drums like a rock star.' Glenda's thumb shot out stiffly. A sigh from me.

She was becoming exasperated. 'And …' she continued, forgetting her fingers in a heated effort to bring me to my senses, 'and … as well as all that, he cares enough about his drunken mates to clean them up, get them home and make sure there is no mess in your grandfather's car.'

'I know. I know.'

'No, you don't,' she said indignantly. 'You don't know how awful guys can be. Believe me, I do! Come down to the club some time and I'll show you what they're like when they grow up a bit. Look, scientists should be cloning this bloke's DNA. Every girl on the planet should get one at least once in her life. Should be standard issue on your eighteenth birthday.'

I sat there like an idiot. Maybe I *was* an idiot.

'Is he going to ask you out again?'

'He rang this morning to thank me for going out with him.'

'HE RANG YOU THE NEXT MORNING!' (The capitals are because she was shouting.) 'I've *got* to meet this guy.' Glenda raised her eyes to the ceiling then twiddled her fingers to show that she had run out of places to count all Todd's good points. 'Rosie Sinclair, your hormones need a good talking-to.'

I deserved that telling-off. What more could a girl ask for? It had been a great night out with Todd. I had really, really enjoyed myself. Who could dream of a better date? So what, if at the end of it all he kisses me like I was his Auntie Rose from the nursing home? It was only a first date. If he had been all over me I would have had to fend him off, and that would have been embarrassing, and he wouldn't have been able to ring me in the morning except to apologise, and then I would have had the upper hand in the relationship and I didn't really want that anyway.

What am I saying? Just rambling, I suppose. I just wish he'd been a bit more ... God, I don't know.

On Monday afternoon, the Duvals wanted to go to the cemetery. I thought that maybe at their age it was fun to pick out a nice spot to lay your bones for the big sleep, but I was ashamed of this thought when I found out the real reason for the visit. They'd had two children, and both of them had 'gone on ahead of them'. That was how Mrs Duval put it. Their son Robert had died of cancer at fifty-one, but as if that wasn't tragic enough, on the other side of the cemetery they showed me the gravestone of Elise, their daughter. I did a little sum in my head, subtracting the year of birth from the year of death.

'She was only twenty-three.'

Mr Duval nodded. 'Died in a rock fall in Switzerland,' he explained. 'She'd only been married a year. Her husband took her on a kind of late honeymoon, hiking through the Alps.'

'Should have stayed at home,' said Mrs Duval, as though she were still arguing over such a silly idea for a honeymoon after all these years.

On the way out, they stopped to say hello to a few old friends who had also gone on ahead of them. Jack, Freda, Laurie, old Graham Decker. No wonder they needed me to drive them around. No children still alive and all their mates underground. Why did Grandad try to warn me about these two old dears? 'Just be discreet,' he said. Discreet about what? If their lives were any more discreet they could take up residence in this cemetery right now.

After I had dropped the Duvals home I noticed the Merc was low on petrol. Grandad had said something about a petrol station in Pine Street. It wasn't far, so I steered in that direction and soon found the sign, *Ferguson's Auto Centre*. It must be the last independent servo left on Earth, and to be honest, it looked as if a strong gust of wind could carry it off to heaven. Most people in Prestwidge buy their petrol from the big glossy places with their flashy signs and gaudy colours. Ferguson's was a kind of oil-stain grey.

There were cars everywhere, lined up one behind the other in the street outside or parked off the road, only inches apart, in every little nook and cranny. They were like patients waiting to be taken into surgery, though in this case the operations were carried out in a dim and rather filthy workshop by men in even filthier overalls. As I brought the Merc to a halt beside a bowser, I saw that a driveway led up the side of the workshop and onto an apron of concrete, where even more cars were having their entrails examined.

Make no mistake. This was Petrol Head City. Bloke Heaven. Absolutely No Chicks Allowed. Didn't bother me, though. I didn't plan to stay long.

The thing about independent servos is, well, the service. Not that I had realised this yet. I had climbed out of the car, still in my school uniform, when a guy came to fill the tank for me. I didn't notice him until he called out to me. 'I'll do that for you,' he said.

'No, it's OK. I can …' I looked up from the bowser. BANG. It was like a karate kick in the chest, right through to my heart. He was wearing jeans over leather ankle boots and a T-shirt that fitted tightly across his abs and around his biceps. His hair spilled out behind his ears, all bronze and gold curls, the ends just brushing his shoulders, one of which was adorned with a fetching smear of grease where he had wiped his hand. His chin was strong, its lines faintly blurred by a day or two's growth, just enough to make it look intentional.

Oh, boy! Smile, smile. Were the muscles of my face doing the right thing?

He seemed to be waiting for something. At last, he reached forward. 'May I?' He took the nozzle from my hand.

I think I said something intelligible. Maybe I just said, 'Thanks.'

He turned away to the car and slid the nozzle into place. This gave me a chance to look down at myself, to make sure everything was in place. Shit, my school uniform, an outfit deliberately designed by witches to make girls look ugly enough to crack mirrors. Why hadn't I gone home and changed?

My eyes hurried back to that body. I didn't think guys wore jeans like that outside old cowboy movies. A flick of his head tossed the curls out of the way. I think my heart missed three beats. Did I sigh? I hoped not, but I must have made some sound, because he turned his head towards me and smiled absently without parting his lips. It wasn't just that he was good-looking … I put my hand on the door of the Mercedes to steady myself.

'You can get back into the car if you like. I'll take care of everything.'

'No. It's fine. I like standing.'

Yes! I actually said that. *I like standing.* What a moron!

'Would you like me to look under your bonnet?'

Oh, you bet, mister, but he meant the car of course. 'Er, yeah, sure.'

My eyes followed him to the front of the Mercedes. Again he hesitated, staring patiently at me. Blue eyes. Definitely blue.

'You have to pull the handle inside the car to release the bonnet,' he said.

'Oh, right.' Idiot. I did as he asked and moments later my view was blocked by the stupid bonnet. I moved to the side and watched as he checked the oil and the water and whatever.

'I've seen this car round the place. Old bloke was driving it.'

'That's my grandad. He's letting me drive it while he's ... out of town.'

'Lucky you. Great piece of machinery. Classic lines.' He stood back admiring the Mercedes. I hoped he might notice some other classic lines and turned a little to give him my best angle. It was hopeless. Bloody school uniform. Even Glenda had looked like a dag in this, so what chance did I have?

I took off into the office to see about paying — or not paying if Grandad had told me the truth. The gorgeous guy strolled casually away like he owned the entire world and it was time for an inspection.

'Well, hello. It's Rosie, isn't it?' I turned away from the window to find a much older man beaming at me. 'You're Paddy's girl.'

'Granddaughter,' I said. This must be Fergo, I decided. 'Grandad told me I could get his car filled up while he's ...'

The smile disappeared from Fergo's face. 'How's he doing in there?' he asked solemnly.

I gave him some equally solemn reassurance. It was like talking about a death in the family — which it was, I suppose, though at least Grandad would come back to life after six months.

'Look, er, there's no charge for the petrol,' Fergo told me.

'Are you sure? It seemed to take quite a lot.'

'No worries. Your grandad used to take my mother over to the quack every week before she passed away.'

This didn't surprise me at all. I stared out of the window again towards the black Mercedes. 'Mr Ferguson,' I said, careful to sound casual, 'who's the guy...' Oh, dear. What was his job? What did you call them? '... the one who pumps the petrol for you?'

Fergo looked out through the grimy window, but there was no-one to be seen. 'Could be any one of my fellas. What did he look like?'

I gave Fergo a verbal sketch but it left him puzzled. 'Sounds like a male model the way you describe him. The only young bloke I've got here is my grandson, Darren, and he's as ugly as a sack full of ...' When he realised he was talking to a girl and not some grease-stained mechanic, he left the sentence unfinished. 'Oh, now, wait on. I know who you mean. Yeah, me sister's grandson. He hangs round here a bit, working on his own car. He's got a good pair of hands, actually.'

I bet he does. I was wondering about that myself, though maybe not in quite the same way. 'Does he have a name?'

Fergo straightened up and looked through the glass again as another car pulled up. 'Chris,' he answered, surprised that anyone should be so interested. 'Chris Meagher.'

NINE

THERE WAS A MESSAGE FROM Glenda waiting for me when I got home. It said that she had something to tell me which she didn't want to discuss over the phone. And I *definitely* had something to tell her.

As soon as I had changed out of my uniform, I headed over to her place, which she shares with two other girls, Sharon and Willie (short for Wilhelmina). Oh, here we go. I can never remember which is which. I think Sharon is a dentist's receptionist who could do with a make-over and Willie is a beautician with really bad teeth. Or is it the other way round? Under the circumstances, a little confusion is natural, I reckon. One day I won't be able to stop myself. I'm going to say to Willie, *Why don't you get Sharon's dentist to fix your teeth?* Or maybe I'll point out to Sharon that she shares a house with a *beautician* and could perhaps ask a little favour …

Neither Sharon nor Willie was home, so Glenda answered my knock. OK, maybe I could have played the situation with a little more cool, but it's easy to be wise after the event. The look on my face was probably visible on radar anyway.

'I've just seen the most *gorgeous* guy,' I said breathlessly before I was even through the door.

Glenda rolled her eyes. 'I know. You kissed him and turned him into a frog.'

'No, not Todd. This is a new guy. His name's Chris Meagher.'

Glenda was walking ahead of me down the hall towards her room but when she heard the name, she stopped dead in her tracks. I was too excited to pay much attention. I swept straight past her and into her bedroom, prattling on about the petrol station and his curls and those jeans. Then I finally realised she didn't seem that impressed.

Come on, Glenda, play the game, I felt like saying to her. What's the point of feeling like a marshmallow inside if your best friend doesn't want to hear about it?

'I know him,' she said finally, and in a rather flat voice. 'He was in my class at school for years.'

'Was he as hot then as he is now?'

'He was hot,' she said, with more eye-rolling.

Despite these words, Glenda had definitely gone

cold on my story. I gave up. 'What did you want to tell me about, anyway?' I asked her.

Her mood changed instantly. She closed the door of her room, even though her housemates weren't even home, then sat on the end of her bed, which creaked on its springs. Sharon and Willie had moved in first, so they had the better bedrooms. The landlord was always promising her a bed that didn't sag but never came through. 'You mentioned a ring the other day, right? Something to do with your grandfather?'

It was a huge change of topic, but I managed to drag my thoughts away from tight T-shirts and curls long enough to nod.

Glenda lowed her voice even further. 'I asked around at the club on Saturday night, but no-one had heard about a missing ring. Then this morning, before I went to uni, one of the bouncers called me. His name's Mick. He fancies me, I think. (So what else is new?) Anyway, he'd made a few inquiries on his own to try and impress me, and he heard about this robbery, going back weeks ago. A jewellery store on Gresham Street was knocked over.'

Ring. Jewellery. It wasn't hard to see the connection. And Glenda had done more than just make the connection. She had dates and specific details to pass on. 'When was your grandfather arrested?' she asked.

I didn't exactly know the date off by heart. 'Hang on. It was the day I helped Mum out at the salon because Tracey had to get one of her ex-husbands out on bail.' (That's Prestwidge for you. We all know where the police lock-up is.)

When we checked a calendar, the dates matched. 'It was the same night!' I said, becoming excited. 'It *must* have something to do with this guy on the phone. He thinks Grandad is fencing the stolen jewellery!'

But before I could speculate any further, Glenda threw a spanner in the works. 'They got all the stuff back, though. The diamonds or whatever, all of it?'

'You mean they caught the thief?'

'Sort of. The cops are pretty sure it's a man named McWhirter. Trouble is, the poor guy's in hospital, in a coma.'

'A coma!'

'That's what Mick said. He was hit by a drunk on a push-bike. Silly fool was riding it on the footpath, middle of the night, no lights, dodgy brakes, and *whack*, this McWhirter falls and hits his head.'

Only in Prestwidge!

'And he had the jewels on him.'

'No, not a thing, but he's got a record as long as your arm, apparently, and the cops have him pinned as the prime suspect.'

'So how did they get the diamonds back?'

'Found them. They were all in a plastic bag the cops discovered on a vacant block near the jewellery store. According to Mick, the thief botched the job and had police coming from everywhere. He must have panicked when he heard the sirens and tossed the bag away in case the police nabbed him.'

'But if all the stuff was recovered, why is that nasty voice calling Grandad's mobile?'

Good question. No answers. After a pause, Glenda asked, 'Do you think you should call the cops?'

'What, me? Paddy Larkin's granddaughter? He'd drum me out of the family!'

'But they might know something Mick couldn't tell me.'

She had a point, but it's never that easy for someone in my family. 'I can't just waltz into the police station and start asking questions. What if Grandad *did* steal a ring somewhere along the line? He could end up in gaol for six *years* instead of six *months*.'

'We'll phone them, then. Anonymously.'

'They can trace calls straightaway these days. Even pizza places can do it.'

'We're talking about the cops here,' Glenda pointed out. 'They're not as smart as the guys at pizza places.'

That was true, but I still thought we should be careful.

'We'll phone from a call box, then.' There was one on the corner, not far from Glenda's, and surprise, surprise, it hadn't been vandalised yet since the last time they fixed it. I rang the number and asked for the detective who was on the jewellery store case. A few clicks later a heavy male voice said, 'Yeah, Morgan.'

What should I say? I hesitated. 'Oh, um, I wanted to know about that jewel robbery a couple of weeks back.'

'You want to know about it. What do you mean?'

This was terrible. The guy thought I was an idiot. 'I'd like to know some details.'

'Details! Listen, what's your name, for a start?'

Name. Oh, God. 'Er...' I looked around. 'Giselle.'

Glenda's eyes just about exploded out of their sockets. 'What are you doing?' she hissed. 'There's cops in the club all the time, getting a free peek. He'll recognise my name.'

The policeman hadn't heard this. In fact, he didn't want to hear much at all. 'You expect me to believe your name's Giselle? Look, little honey, you don't sound so old to me. If this is some kind of joke, I've got better things to do.'

'No, no. I'm serious. I need to know about the stuff that was stolen in that robbery.'

'That information is confidential. If you're doing a school project, you should find some topic that doesn't waste people's time.'

'Was all the jewellery found? They say it was recovered on the night of the robbery.'

'Well, whoever "they" are was right. Now, if you'll excuse me ...'

'No, wait. Is there a ring still missing?'

Now it was the detective's turn to hesitate. 'Why did you ask that?'

'Well, was there?' I asked bluntly, feeling a little more confident now. His voice had changed, as though he wasn't quite so ready to get rid of me.

'Now, listen, young lady. If you *have* found a ring somewhere, you should hand it in to the police.'

I stayed quiet.

'You *have* found something, haven't you? Would you like to describe the ring to me?'

'So there *is* a ring still missing from that robbery?'

He thought about his answer for a moment. 'Yes,' he said finally. 'Now, if you will just describe the ring you've found, I can tell you if it's the one we're looking for.'

'No, thanks,' I said lightly, as though I had just ordered a meat lovers' with extra pepperoni then changed my mind. 'I've found out all I wanted to know.'

I put the phone back on the hook.

'So there *is* a missing ring,' said Glenda, once I'd closed the door of the phone booth behind me.

I nodded slowly while I tried to work things out.

'Your grandad wasn't in on that robbery, was he?'

'Of course not.'

'Well, whoever is making those calls on your mobile thinks he was.'

'No, he couldn't have had anything to do with it. He was off shifting gear for Bruce that night. He'd borrowed a van and everything.'

'Where was his car, then?'

'I don't know. Parked outside his mate's place until he came back with the van, I suppose.'

'And where was that?'

I threw my hands in the air. 'Glenda, how would *I* know?'

'Don't get shirty,' she snapped. 'What I'm saying is, maybe the Mercedes is part of this.'

I was about to tell her she was crazy when the penny finally dropped. 'The cigarette smoke,' I whispered.

'What?'

'Don't you remember? I told you about it days ago. I took the Duvals shopping, and when we came back to the car there was a smell of cigarette smoke inside.'

'So someone must have broken into the Mercedes after all. Did they take anything?'

'Nothing to steal except the car itself, and there wasn't any sign that they'd tried it. They must have just been searching it.'

'For that ring?'

'It looks like it now, doesn't it?'

By this time, we were back at Glenda's place, where the Mercedes was parked in the driveway. She started on the passenger side, I searched the driver's side. Nothing under the seats or in the crevice between the cushions. Nothing hidden behind the dash.

'What about the boot?'

'It would've been locked.'

'Yeah, but if they could get into the car, they could get into the boot, don't you reckon?'

I opened the boot for the first time since Grandad had given me the keys. Nothing.

'They've been in here, though, searching,' said

Glenda. She leaned forward and pointed to a crease mark running diagonally across the corner of the carpet that lined the boot. Tiny pieces of grit had collected in the crease when it was folded back, making the line easily visible. There was hard evidence, then, that I wasn't dreaming or making things up. This was as real as that sinister voice on Grandad's mobile.

Glenda and I searched under the carpet and in the tool kit, then checked out the wheel jack, then went back to the interior to try again. It was at that point, with Glenda going through the glove box and me in the back seat, that it hit me. Uncle Bruce! Now I knew why I'd found him in the back seat of Grandad's car. He wasn't trying to steal it, I said to myself. He was searching it too.

I told Glenda about how Bruce had come to visit us on Saturday. 'He knows something,' Glenda said with a sly grin on her face.

'The bastard,' I muttered. We went back inside Glenda's house and I rang his number. No answer. Just his machine, asking me to leave a message. 'You mongrel,' I said then put down the phone. He wouldn't be able to work out it was me — and I'll bet I wasn't the first person to leave a message like that for Bruce Larkin.

TEN

DON'T YOU JUST HATE IT when you end up getting busted by accident? I mean, if you're going to cop a blast from an irate teacher or a mother who's frothing at the mouth, then at least you should get the chance to enjoy whatever you're meant to have done wrong in the first place.

I left Grandad's mobile on in class, didn't I? It was Tuesday morning and I'd taken a call from the Eisenberg sisters before school. Without realising it, I'd slipped the phone back into the pocket of my uniform without turning it off. Next thing I know, I'm in Mr Tudor's Science class when the damn thing starts to vibrate against my thigh, and before I can react, it starts to squeal. I tried to fish the phone out of my pocket, and because I was so embarrassed and in such a hurry, I fumbled it badly. By the time I had it properly in my hands, it had rung five times and the whole class was in an uproar.

Mr Tudor even thought I was going to answer it. He went ballistic. Can't say that I blame him, really, with the rest of the class laughing and cheering like I'd just scored some big-time hit to make fun of him.

'Out!' he shouted. 'Go and see Mr Hoskins and maybe you can explain to him how you have the temerity to disrupt my lesson.'

How can teachers tell you off in such perfect English? I trudged down to the office and told the secretary I had to see the Deputy Principal.

'Join the queue,' she said. Sarcastic bitch.

I sat down beside two unbearably smug Year Nines with the skirts of their uniforms hitched up to look like micro-minis. They reeked of stale cigarettes, which in view of my recent experiences didn't endear them to me much.

'What'd *you* do?' one of them asked.

'I stabbed two chicks for blowing smoke in my face,' I answered. It took a moment or two before they worked out I just might be exaggerating.

The door opened and the nicotine-drenched pair sauntered off to their fate. But it wasn't all bad. There, on the chipped and unsteady coffee table in front of me, lay a mess of school annuals. If Chris Meagher had been in Glenda's class, then ... I found the right year and flicked through impatiently until there it was, an individual photo, in alphabetical order. He looked so young, and of course his hair was shorter, but all this made him even cuter. Under the portrait his name was spelled out. Not *Chris* or *Christopher*. His full name was *Christian Meagher*. I loved it.

I searched for him among the sports teams. Football, basketball. He looked even better in a singlet and shorts, with those muscles fully on show.

There were informal photos scattered through the pages as well, snapshots taken at dances and on school camps. There he was in one shot, at the centre of a group gathered round a picnic table. He was giving the camera a roguish glare that demanded the world take him seriously. But this wasn't what I noticed first about that picture. No, sir. Another face caught my eye before his did. A very familiar face. Glenda was sitting beside him, and around her waist, holding her tightly against him, was the arm of Christian Meagher.

The door to Mr Hoskins' office opened again. Out came the two girls, though this time there was no swagger in their step. Both faces had gone white and one of them had been crying. She still was, I realised, when I heard her sniffling pathetically into the back of her hand. In spite of my contempt for both of them, my mouth went suddenly dry.

Then Mr Hoskins appeared behind them to see if there were any more miscreants to be reduced to tears. Time to describe Mr Hoskins. I think the best way is this. Make a list of everything that has ever been said about deputy principals, even the outrageous stuff that is obviously a huge exaggeration. Inspect the list. Cross out anything that seems the least bit positive, friendly or helpful. What's left probably describes Mr Hoskins. Without exaggeration. As for appearance, well, let's just say he resembles a toad with glasses and leave it at that.

'Rosie Sinclair. I haven't had the pleasure of your company for … let's see … nearly a month. Is it sheer laziness, or did the Good Fairy touch you with her wand?'

Mr Hoskins has just the best line in sarcasm. I hope to be as good as him one day. I mean, you go to school to learn *useful* stuff, don't you?

'Inside,' he growled. The door clicked shut behind us and my mouth became a desert. 'So what have you been up to?'

'My mobile went off in Mr Tudor's class, Sir,' I said contritely. 'I'm sorry, really I am.' I find it easier just to grovel and get it over with unless there is some question of principle involved.

Mr Hoskins seemed pleased that he had me pleading forgiveness without his lifting a finger. 'Not the worst crime that's been paraded before me today,' he said, a little bored. 'Perhaps Mr Tudor could have had a little more patience.'

Phew! I was going to get off without a detention! But then the phone rang. Not his phone. Mine. I'd put it back in my pocket again, but with Mr Tudor yelling at me and the class smirking and applauding, I must have forgotten to turn it off.

I looked at Mr Hoskins. Not such a crime, my face was trying to say, but that brief moment of calm and understanding on his had vanished. He gave me a look that told me what I already knew. I was a fool. What's more, as soon as I had the phone out of my pocket, he snatched it from my hand. 'Let *me* handle this. I'd like to know who thinks they can call up a schoolgirl in the middle of lessons.' He stabbed at the Answer button. 'Hello?'

Oh, God. What if it was one of my oldies. They'd have a heart attack.

But it was worse. Much worse. '*What* ring?' spat Mr Hoskins, and instantly I knew who was calling.

'Don't you threaten me,' said Mr Hoskins, raising his voice. 'Believe me, I've been threatened by experts and I won't be intimidated by you.'

'Mr Hoskins, please,' I said rather sheepishly, but he took no notice.

'What's that?' he asked into the phone. 'What did you call me? Paddy! I'm no Irishman. Who *is* this?'

I considered snatching the phone back, but that might get me suspended or even expelled. Luckily Mr Hoskins now decided he'd had enough. He ended the call then turned off the phone. 'You have some rude boyfriends, Rosie. That one sounded old enough to be your father. Do you have any idea who it was?'

'A wrong number, maybe?' I suggested, shrugging my shoulders weakly.

He gave me a thunderous look. 'Wrong number, indeed. I'll keep this phone for the rest of the day. You can pick it up at three o'clock, and since you can't seem to learn to turn it off, you'd better keep it at home from now on. *Is that clear?*'

ELEVEN

THAT BLOODY MOBILE! I THOUGHT about leaving it there, in the Deputy Principal's office. Switching it off for good. Or letting the battery run down. That sinister voice wouldn't be able to reach me then. Neither would all those old people who had me driving them around Prestwidge as though I were their own personal taxi driver.

But that was just it. I couldn't let those dear old things fend for themselves. How would Mrs Foat see her dying sister? How would the Duvals get down to the shops? Besides, I liked them.

So I went to see the crew from the A List. They were more likely to know about mobiles than anyone. Justine filled me in, and as soon as I retrieved the phone from Mr Hoskins, I put my newfound knowledge into practice. I set up a message bank.

On the way home, I looked at the petrol gauge. Damn. The little needle was still touching 'F'. I drove the long way home. Didn't do much good. Still full. Luckily, I was due to take Mrs Foat to the hospital. While I was waiting to take her home again, I called the Duvals to see how their supplies were going.

'We're a bit low on sugar,' Janice told me, 'but don't worry. We can stretch it out until next week without any bother.' So I took them some sugar.

After a few more completely unnecessary kindnesses like this, by the next afternoon the needle in the petrol gauge had finally fallen a little below the 'F'. Time to ponder a new fashion dilemma. What does a girl wear when buying petrol? I pulled every item out of my wardrobe, one after another, and held each one up against myself in front of the mirror.

No way.

Daggy.

Old maid.

So yesterday.

At last everything I owned lay discarded on my bed. Who was I kidding, anyway? I already knew what I was going to wear. I put on Glenda's skirt and tried to look at myself from behind. Nearly put my neck out. Oh, bugger it. I'll just make sure Chris looks at me from the front. I ironed the same pink top I'd worn to the party on Saturday — it had just been through the wash. As for make-up … well, I thought I was being rather restrained really, until Jason spotted me from the sofa, where he was hibernating for the decade.

'Jesus, look at your face! Did you just win a whole lot of free samples or something?'

That should have been a warning, but did I take the hint? Not Rosie Sinclair.

At Ferguson's garage, I parked the Merc beside the petrol pump and got out eagerly. A gust of wind reminded me how short Glenda's skirt was. Then a figure appeared from the workshop … but it wasn't the one I'd expected. Yuck, pizza features! This must be Darren and he was every bit as repulsive as Fergo had said he was.

'Fillerup?'

I nodded and he went to work.

'Where's your friend?' I asked.

'Friend?'

'He was here on Monday.'

He thought about this for a minute. 'Chris, yeah, he's here. Hey, Chris!' he shouted. A few seconds later, there he was, striding towards me, in a different T-shirt this time but with the same body underneath. 'Hello again,' he said. 'Rosie, is that right?'

I smiled. I think maybe 'I beamed' would be more accurate. He looked at me, that hair dancing lightly around his forehead in the breeze. I wanted to brush it aside for him and see his whole face unobstructed, but before this pleasant little fantasy had gone far, the pump clicked off. Darren adjusted the nozzle, but after another second or two the flow stopped again.

'It's full,' said Darren. He looked at the numbers on the panel. 'Seven dollars sixty. Hardly worth your while coming in.'

'Oh, I was just passing and I thought I might as well have a full tank.'

They glanced at each other and then laughed — at me! In fact, Chris now stood staring at me openly, admiring everything he could see. This was what I had come for, it was why I had squeezed into a skirt one size too small and a hundred miles too short, but it was hardly how I had planned the meeting. That smirk on his face was becoming downright haughty. 'You're Paddy Larkin's granddaughter, aren't you?'

I nodded, hoping this would get a bit of conversation going, but that full-of-himself smile was unsettling me more and more. Then it came to me. He knew my name and who I was because Fergo had told him — and that wasn't all Fergo had said. He must have been told how I'd asked about him on Monday. Oh, God. I was making a total fool of myself. He knew I didn't need petrol. He knew I had come just to see him, and there I was in Glenda's skirt with my face all made-up. What was I *doing*?

I quickly pulled open the driver's door, but as I slipped in behind the wheel that damn skirt rode halfway up to my armpits. Through it all he stood there, watching and chuckling like he was God's gift to women and I had come along to beg for my tiny share of such a wonderful present.

I was furious — with myself, mostly. It was all I could do to keep the Mercedes moving in a straight line. Once I had regained a bit of composure, I realised my mind had already decided on the best course of action. Confession is usually the quickest way to feeling better. I would confess my stupidity to Glenda and let her tell me what an idiot I was. Then I'd get angry with her and forgive myself. It was the perfect system.

Glenda opened the door when she heard my knock then looked me up and down. 'Don't tell me. You've been to audition for my job at the club, right?'

'Shut up,' I said, steaming past her and heading straight for her room.

'I'll get the chocolate,' she called after me in a knowing tone.

That was another reason why the car had steered itself in this direction. Glenda always had a supply of mint chocolate in the fridge. Somehow, she managed to make a mid-sized block last a fortnight, nibbling a piece now and then and even forgetting about it for a week at a time. No stress in her life, that's why. She arrived with two rows, from a family-sized block, my eagle eye noticed. She handed me one row and kept the other.

The chocolate was cold and hard and delicious. I

let the warmth of my mouth thaw it out a little before sinking my teeth into the soft, minty middle. Was there a more comforting sensation in the whole world?

'OK, what did you do?'

I explained.

'You're an idiot,' Glenda announced obligingly.

'But he's gorgeous! How else am I going to make him notice me?'

Glenda should also have obliged me with a deprecating laugh at this point, and that was how it should all have ended. There's nothing like a good laugh to remind us how unimportant boys are in the scheme of things. Instead, she frowned. 'He's a bad one, Rosie. Forget it.'

Well, if she wasn't going to play by the usual rules, I'd change them too. 'I had a look through some old Prestwidge High annuals the other day. Chris's real name is Christian. Did you know that?'

Of course she knew that. She waited, knowing what was yet to come.

'You were in that annual too, Glenda. Sitting next to him.'

'All right. I knew him.'

'Knew him! An anaconda would have had a looser grip round your waist.'

'So we had a thing for a while.'

'What's "a thing"?'

'That's personal.'

'So how long is "a while"?'

'A few months. Look, Rosie, I'm serious. Chris Meagher is bad news. You don't want to get mixed up with him.'

I waited, staring at her.

'That's it. I'm not telling you any more. We went out for a while. We broke up.'

I pressed her, with pursed lips and raised eyebrows, just to see if what she really wanted was for me to make her spill the whole story. But her face hardened. This was one story I wasn't going to hear — not right now, anyway.

I went into the kitchen. In the kitchen was the fridge, and in the fridge was the chocolate. I broke off one more row, looked at the rest of the block in my hand and thought, What the hell? and took the lot back to the bedroom.

The break had given me a chance to think, and I had to admit Glenda was right. Chris Meagher *was* bad news. I mean, how arrogant was he? And how *insulting* to stand there staring me up and down like that!

The trouble was, Glenda's warning still hadn't put me off. If anything, I felt more intrigued — yes, even excited. When I drove out of that service station, I was angry with Chris for his arrogance and his teasing smile, but before I'd reached the end of the street I had started to see things from his point of view. Poor guy. What else was he going to do? I'd gone there to show myself off, just like a thoroughbred at one of those auctions. I should have stamped a lot number on my massive rump. He knew the car didn't need petrol, and he knew I didn't dress in a tight little skirt just to cruise around the suburbs. It was *my* fault, not his.

Glenda watched me closely from across the room. She could read me like a book. 'What about Todd?' she asked me. 'The perfect date?'

'*Almost* perfect,' I responded sharply.

'OK, so the guy needs a few kissing lessons. You could be his tutor.'

I shrugged.

Glenda went on the attack. The hand she had used to count off Todd's good points was up again in front of her face. The fingers twiddled. 'Remember, Rosie, he's got a lot of major pluses in the boyfriend department. You should give him a chance.'

'It wasn't just the kiss. I tried to tell you. There just wasn't any spark.'

'Yeah, and Chris hangs around a petrol station. One spark and you'll go up in a ball of flames.' Her hands flew apart extravagantly.

I knew she was right. 'It's my stupid hormones. They need a good talking-to, like you said.'

'Looks to me like you're a little too keen to take them for a walk round the block. You know what I think? I think I'd better be your leash.'

'No, it's OK. He's not likely to ask me out now, is he?'

'See! You're still thinking about it.'

I was, too.

'Promise me, Rosie. Promise me now. If he ever asks you out, you'll say no.'

I gave her an uncertain glare from beneath hooded eyelids.

'Promise,' she demanded.

'All right, all right. I promise.'

Glenda looked pleased at last.

I looked down at the silver wrapping. Oops. No chocolate left.

TWELVE

I SHOULD HAVE KNOWN WHAT to expect when something so unusual, so completely unprecedented occurred without any kind of warning.

On Thursday, at precisely eight twenty-seven a.m., my brother Jason Sinclair got off the couch. I thought at first he was making a point to Grandma, who had been giving him merry hell about his laziness ever since she moved in with us. She had already cleaned the house from top to bottom, including a thorough vacuuming of the sofa while Jason was still lying on it.

More surprising still, Jason spoke to me in a sentence instead of an incomprehensible gabble of grunts and gestures. 'Rosie, could you do us a favour?' he entreated eloquently.

Of course he wanted something from me, but hey, that's a form of communication too. 'Careful there, Jason,' I warned as he stood in front of me. 'Make sure you're steady on those legs before you try walking. They might have atrophied.'

He didn't have a clue what 'atrophied' meant but he knew from my tone that I was having a go at him. 'Funny girl,' he sneered. 'A real comedian.' Then he remembered he needed a favour and the sneering vanished. 'It's my mate, Ben. He's moving house. He needs a lift with all his gear.'

'The Merc's not a removal van, Jason. Tell him to hire a truck.'

'No, no. He hasn't got any furniture or anything. Just a few bags.'

'You can't borrow the Mercedes.'

'Yeah, I know you're touchy on the subject. Grandad gave it to you to mind and you're gonna take good care of it. I'm cool with that. But maybe you could drive him. There's no buses where he's living now and taxis are, like, *so* expensive.' (Except for Rosie's black taxi, that is.)

Like a fool, I asked where he was living. It was out in the sticks a bit, but not too far. I could open up the throttle on the Merc for a change. When I asked where he was moving to, he knew I would say yes.

'Thanks, Rosie. You're a great sister.' Yeah, a regular girl guide. But I wasn't going to miss any school to do this bloke a favour, not when I was already on the nose with Mr Hoskins.

'That's OK,' said Jason. 'When you get back would be cool.' He stretched out on the couch again so he could rest up for the big adventure.

It was already after four by the time we headed out of Prestwidge with the windows open and the radio turned up as far as it would go. Jason wasn't such bad company when he got off his butt. He dabbled a little with a band that let him sing, and he could keep a note pretty well when he put his mind to it. It was his couch-potato body that let him down.

We were out among some small farms by the time he pointed out the turn-off. They were old, desperately poor and falling down, with rusting machinery dotting the paddocks, and only the occasional pathetic horse or goat watching us as we passed in a cloud of dust, with the motor roaring. Then another turn off, this time onto a rutted track, with even less evidence of civilisation in sight.

'Not far now,' Jason assured me when I complained about damage to the Merc.

He was true to his word, strangely. Another half mile and we were swallowed up by thick forest. In among the trees, a house, or a hut, really — no, not even that, more a shanty — appeared in the shade of some trees. Jason's friend Ben had heard us coming (little wonder) and was already outside waiting, with some bags at his feet. When I got out to meet him, I saw that two of the bags were grubby hold-alls, but the third was just a black plastic garbage bag tied at the top with some adhesive tape. It bulged at the sides.

'What's in there?'

Ben looked down at the black bag, then at Jason, as though he were hoping my brother would answer for him. 'Just clothes and stuff. I didn't have anything else to put 'em in.'

Ben obviously came from the same school of hard work as my brother. I opened the boot and he dumped the two hold-alls carelessly inside. He was more cautious with the plastic bag. I would be too, I suppose. If it split, his few worldly possessions would be all over the place.

Then it was back to civilisation — though that's stretching the word a bit considering it was only Prestwidge we were heading for. I steered away from The Grove and the business district, sticking to the suburban streets.

We were cruising casually along Hedges Avenue when I got the shock of my life. A police siren sounded briefly, right in my ear. In the rear view mirror I could see the patrol car with its lights flashing. 'Shit. They want me to pull over,' I said to the others. 'What have I done?'

What indeed! I was well under the speed limit, all the lights worked, I hadn't run a red light or a Stop sign. I pulled over and scrambled out of the car, aware vaguely that Jason and his mate were doing the same.

Behind us, a cop closed the door of his car and came slowly towards me. I recognised him from Grandad's trial. The one who'd spotted the stolen parkas. Name of Enright.

'What's wrong?' I asked, with an innocence and confusion that I didn't have to fake.

'Nothing, I hope, Miss. It's just that I know this car pretty well and I was surprised to see it on the road.'

'Because the owner's in gaol, you mean?'

He couldn't stop the corners of his mouth from curling up in satisfaction. 'You're Paddy's granddaughter, aren't you? Well, I suppose that explains why you're driving it around. Nice car,' he added, in genuine appreciation.

By now, I had relaxed. This wasn't so bad, then. The cops were just checking that no-one had stolen Grandad's car while he was inside. Considerate of them, really. I tried to weigh up whether I could get away with a sarcastic remark along those lines. I glanced over at the other two to make sure they were creating the right impression. There was my brother staring anywhere but at the policeman, and looking decidedly uncomfortable. His mate Ben had disappeared.

'Where'd your friend go?' Enright asked Jason.

'Who?'

Oh, great. That was the best my stupid brother could come up with. He was going to deny there had been another bloke in the car. Enright might be a copper, but he wasn't entirely stupid. 'Don't play games, son. There were two passengers when I pulled you over. Where's he gone?'

'Oh yeah. Him. Right,' said Jason, as though he had just remembered. I didn't know whether to groan or just cry. 'Er, my mate, yeah, he was in a hurry. He's gone on ahead. On foot.'

That helped me make up my mind. I groaned.

Constable Enright, meanwhile, looked down the road. No sign of the missing passenger, and of course now he was suspicious. He came closer and stared into the back seat, expecting to find someone crouched out of sight. This gave me a moment to slip round to where Jason was standing — or rather hopping from one leg to another as though he were a three-year-old desperate for a pee.

'Where's Ben?' I whispered.

'He took off.'

'I know that, you idiot. What's going on?'

'He was afraid the copper would look in the boot.'

The boot! It took me exactly one and a half seconds to make the connection. 'That bag. What the hell's in it?'

Jason gave me a worried look. That was nothing compared with the look I gave him. 'Tell me,' I hissed menacingly.

'It's just some leaves.'

'What kind of leaves?'

The frown became a pathetic wince. 'Grass,' he whispered.

'Grass clippings! What's he carrying grass clippings for?

'No, not *that* kind of grass,' he breathed in exasperation.

At last I understood. 'Mari —' I managed to stop myself just in time, because I had sort of raised my voice a little — which was hardly surprising under the circumstances. I forced my voice into a whisper again and said, 'You let your mate put a squillion bucks' worth of dope into Grandad's car, with me driving it?'

He offered a pathetic look as his reply.

'And now the bastard's taken off.'

'Yeah, well. He can't afford to get caught, can he? Be third offence for him.'

Constable Enright had finally satisfied himself that our friend wasn't hiding in the car. He called me round to his side. 'What's your name?'

I told him politely, hoping he would just go away. Who was I kidding?

'Well, Rosie,' he said. 'I wasn't thinking of searching your car when I pulled you over, but since this mysterious third person has run off, it's all starting to look a bit dodgy. I'd like to look in the boot if you don't mind.'

Oh, great. And what will he find? Two hold-alls with a bunch of unwashed rags belonging to Ben somebody and a black bag stuffed full of strong-smelling leaves. *What's that?* he'll ask.

Oh, nothing special, Constable. Just a little marijuana. You probably enjoy a joint yourself now and again, eh? They'd have me in a cell next door to Grandad before I could blink.

I looked back at Jason. He was no help. He was standing there looking like a condemned prisoner at the foot of the gallows. Think quickly! Think quickly! Oh God, I wish I were good under pressure.

I looked up at Enright, who was being remarkably patient through all this. 'Open the boot, please,' he said calmly.

I couldn't let it happen. Once that boot was open, we were finished.

'This is police harassment,' I said.

He look at me as though I'd farted.

'Harassment,' I said again. Then I just let the words come, don't ask me where they came from. 'I haven't done anything wrong,' I said, louder this time as I warmed up. 'There I was, just driving these guys ...' (oops) '... my brother round the place, well under the speed limit, and you pulled me over for nothing at all. It's not fair, you know. Just because my grandfather has a criminal record doesn't mean that the rest of the family is like that (except for Uncle Bruce, of course). I might be driving Grandad's car, but that doesn't mean I'm involved in crime, does it?'

Constable Enright continued to look at me rather strangely. His expression said, *Where is all this coming from?* Out loud, he said, 'I just want to look in the boot.'

'The boot. You want to look in the boot. Well, where's your search warrant?' Search warrant! Hey, that was good. Must be all those TV shows you can hardly avoid when you're growing up. Yeah, I knew my rights. They had to have a search warrant to go hunting in the boot of your car.

'I don't need a search warrant to look in your boot.'

'Oh, don't you?' I said, disappointed. So much for TV shows.

'No, not if I have reasonable cause, and since one of your passengers has run off suspiciously, I have all the cause I need to think maybe you're hiding something illegal.'

'Now, there you go again,' I raged. 'Illegal! What right have you got to accuse me of doing something illegal? I'm still at school, you know. Just a schoolgirl. What would an innocent schoolgirl be doing with something illegal in her boot?'

'I don't know,' said the policeman, exasperated. 'Until I see in the boot, I'm not going to know if you're carrying anything illegal in the first place.'

'There you go again. It's all about poor Paddy Larkin, isn't it? Once the cops have got you, they never let go. They stick you in gaol for hardly anything at all and then they start harassing your family.' I went on like this for a full minute, repeating everything I had said before. All the time I was desperately hoping that something would fall from the heavens to save me, but it didn't. I was just putting off the inevitable and making Enright mighty mad at the same time.

'Just get out the keys and let me see inside the boot,' he demanded, losing patience rapidly.

By this time I had worked myself up into an absolute frenzy, more because of Jason than the poor copper. You can't open the boot. That one truth kept hammering away in my brain. The keys, you can't let him have the keys, or he'll open the boot himself.

The keys were in my pocket. I pressed my palm gingerly against them and heard the jingle. 'The keys?' I shouted, hoping that this too would bring some solution. 'You want the keys? Well, OK, if you want the keys, here they are!' I pulled them out of my pocket and looked at them, glinting and heavy in my hand. 'If you want them, then there, you go and get them!' And with a huge heave, I tossed them as hard as I could over Jason's head, towards the footpath. Maybe a serpent would rise up out of the ground and swallow them. Maybe an alien spaceship would swoop down from the sky and carry them off to Jupiter.

We stood there, all three of us, just watching the keys fly through the air. In my desperation, my fear, my anger, I had found more strength than I knew I had. They sailed high over my brother's head, then higher still, then finally began to arc downwards. Just as I expected to see them fall with a clang on the footpath, they disappeared.

'Shit, Rosie! They've gone over the fence!' said Jason.

It was a high fence, too, with wooden palings looming at least two metres tall, each sharpened to a point. Even so, the tops of overgrown trees sprouted thickly above them.

'This is ridiculous. What the hell have you got hidden in that boot? The way you're going on, you'd think it was a dead body.' Yeah, mine! 'What could be so important?'

'It's the principle,' I announced self-righteously.

'Principle, my arse. You're hiding something. Now, you go and find those keys!' He was furious now.

I folded my arms. 'You want them, *you* go get them.'

'Get those keys, or I'll arrest you!' he threatened.

What the hell. If he found that bag of dope he would arrest me anyway. 'Go right ahead. But you'll still be the one who has to find my keys.' Did I really say that? It was all a bluff, of course. If he took a single step towards me I would probably start crying like a baby and beg him to let me go.

But it seemed I had made him think again. The good constable had no intention of scaling that fence and scrambling about in the undergrowth to find the keys. I can work up a fairly determined pout when I try, and he could tell I wasn't going to do it either. He glared at me. I glared at him. We were like two gunslingers in an old western on TV.

Then he noticed Jason, idling about helplessly. 'You!' he bellowed. 'Find those keys.'

'Me? I didn't throw them in there.'

Police tempers are not renowned for being generous, and unlike me, Jason didn't have a pout that could frighten rhinos. His most determined look is more a plea for mercy. It didn't work on Enright. He took a few threatening steps towards my brother and Jason suddenly changed his mind. 'All right, all right.'

He backed away towards the gate. It was an equally high affair, built of the same rough palings. Attached to this gate was a faded sign. *Enter At Own Risk.*

'Hey, look at this. What's it mean, do you think?'

'They've probably got a Rottweiler,' said Constable Enright, smiling grimly, and he wasn't far wrong. Alsatian. I could see it through the gaps in the palings. Looked hungry, too.

'Well that's that,' said Jason with relief. 'If I go in there, I'll be ripped to pieces.'

'If you stay out here you'll be ripped to pieces,' was the policeman's reply.

I didn't hear the rest of this conversation. A Ford utility had pulled up across the road. I turned to give the driver a *mind your own business* glare, then gulped. It was Chris Meagher, and he was already out of the ute and heading across the road towards me.

THIRTEEN

'WHAT'S GOING ON, ROSIE?'

'I've lost my keys,' I said.

'Where'd they go?'

I nodded towards the fence, where the policeman and my brother were still arguing over how to get the keys from an Alsatian-infested yard.

Chris looked puzzled. 'How can you lose your keys over a fence like that — and what's Enright doing here, anyway?'

I was still embarrassed by my last meeting with Chris Meagher. At first I had just wanted him to go away, but I was desperate, and after all, doesn't a drowning person cling onto any buoy that comes along? (Sorry, that's an accidental pun, but come to think of it, this expresses my feelings at the time quite well.)

In as few words as possible, and with my voice low in case a certain word escaped too loudly, I explained.

He laughed. (Bastard.) Then he thought about it all and that huge smile disappeared. 'Actually, you're in deep shit.'

'Thanks for saying that.'

'What are you going to do?'

'I'm hoping to die in the next few minutes. Other than that, I don't have a plan.'

On the footpath, the struggle continued, joined now by the incessant barking of the Alsatian from behind the fence. God, look at the size of it. I'd seen racehorses smaller than that dog.

'If he finds that dope in your boot, you'll end up down at the lock-up. You don't have another key on you, by any chance?'

'Of course not.'

'Well then, we'll have to find another way.'

I was about to ask him what the hell he was talking about when Enright called to me from the gate. 'Get over here, young lady. Look at the trouble you've caused.'

He hadn't even noticed Chris. I looked over my shoulder as I took my time across the footpath and all I could see was Chris heading back to his car. Well, great. Seems we didn't create enough entertainment for Mr Golden Curls.

The details of what followed are hazy in my mind. I know that Jason did eventually go into the yard to get the keys. He wasn't mauled, because Constable Enright is a bit of a dog lover, and he managed to calm the vicious beast down enough to slip one loop of his handcuffs round the collar and lock the dog to the gatepost. There was a lot of growling and shouting, and whether he did it on purpose or not I don't know, but he lost control of the Alsatian just long enough for Jason to get bitten on the butt as he was scuttling through the gate with the keys. He clutched at his jeans and hopped around howling as though the dog had ripped his entire leg off. What a baby. I couldn't see any blood. No blood, no sympathy, as far as I'm concerned, and the good constable was laughing so hard I thought he was having convulsions.

So the keys were back in our hands. Well, Constable Enright's hands, anyway. He had snatched them from Jason as he was unsuccessfully avoiding those gnashing teeth. 'OK, let's see what you two are so keen to hide,' he said triumphantly.

How long do you get for possession of marijuana? I was wondering. What would Mum say? What about Grandad? He was always telling us to stay away from anything illegal like that. But I was all out of ideas. There was nothing I could do now to stop Enright from opening the boot. Once he knew what was in that black bag, my life was over. I'd end up with a police record. Everyone in Prestwidge would know about Rosie the dope dealer. I started to shake, as though the temperature had suddenly dropped below zero. This was SERIOUS!

We followed the constable back to the car, and that was when I noticed Chris Meagher hadn't left after all.

'What are *you* doing here, Meagher?' Constable Enright growled. Hey, these two know each other, I realised, and it didn't sound like a terribly friendly relationship.

'I'm a friend of Rosie's,' he answered confidently. 'I was just passing and wondered what the trouble was.'

'Well, stay right back. This is none of your business.'

Unfortunately, it was *my* business, though. I stood watching as the key was fitted into the lock and the lid of the boot swung upwards. We all stared inside, except Chris, who had backed off a few metres towards the ute. I looked at Jason. His mouth was hanging open. Maybe mine was too. We closed them quickly, as soon as Enright turned to us.

'That's it? Two bags? What's in them?' He pulled the two hold-alls out of the boot. There was no black plastic bag. It had simply vanished. I looked at Chris Meagher, who was doing his best to look surprised himself.

Enright searched both bags. It would be more accurate to say he pulled all the clothes out of them and left the contents strewn all over the roadside. 'I don't get it! Why all this fuss over a few clothes?'

'It's the principle,' I said again.

He stood up, with his hands over his kidneys,

staring all around him. He was thoroughly pissed off with the whole affair by this time, and when a policeman is mad, someone has to pay. There is always a crime around somewhere, some law that has been broken.

That was when he spotted the black plastic bag. It hadn't vanished after all but had somehow transported itself, by magic, to a comfortable spot next to a wheelie bin on the footpath. 'Look at this,' said Enright, disgusted. 'Can you believe it? People are told over and over and over again, don't leave rubbish on the footpath like this for the dogs to rip open. Honestly, the mess! People have no consideration!'

He walked over to the bag and picked it up. 'Bloody disgrace,' he muttered as he lifted the lid of the wheelie bin to put the bag inside. But he was frustrated here, too. The lid was already resting on a garbage bag that protruded from the bin like a tennis ball in the mouth of a puppy. The bag of weed was simply too big and bulky. The lid wouldn't rest on top of it and fell back loudly against the body of the bin, and the black bag itself kept rolling off. Each time it hit the ground I held my breath, expecting it to split open.

'Shit!' Enright exploded when the bag fell off a third time. The poor man looked a bit defeated. Not his day, obviously.

Chris Meagher stepped forward. 'You're right,' he said. 'I keep seeing rubbish like this all over the place. A disgrace, just like you said, Constable. Look,

Rosie,' he said, turning to me. 'If you're so full of principle, then you should help out. You can take that bag up to the industrial bin behind Jimmy Way's.' He pointed along Hedges Avenue towards the run-down shop owned by a lethargic Chinese family since before my mother was born.

Enright saw his chance for a little revenge against me. 'Good point,' he said, brightening up a little. 'Are you going to be a civic-minded citizen and get rid of this bag for me, Rosie?'

'Of course she will,' said Chris. 'Only sounds fair, if you ask me, after all the trouble she's caused.'

He took the bag from where it had fallen for the third time, strode right passed Constable Enright and placed it in the boot of the Mercedes. Meanwhile Jason had managed to gather his mate's clothes, along with a lot of dirt and stones, and stuff them back into the hold-alls. More activity than he'd had in a year! He dumped these into the boot as well, and I closed it up with a deep sense of relief.

'Say hello to Paddy for me when you see him,' Enright called as he returned to his car. He was sneering as he said it — his idea of a parting insult. Then he left, in a shower of dust and grit, as he spun his wheels in the gravel.

Jason and I stood watching him go and only when the police car was out of sight along the tree-lined avenue did we turn back to Chris.

How had he done it? He certainly hadn't sprung the lock. That would have been too risky, and if

Enright had seen him from the gate he would have been in more trouble than we were.

Chris smiled and shook his head, rustling those curls. Oh, boy. I went weak at the knees. He pulled a socket wrench from his back pocket and held it up, while with his other hand he invited us to peer into the car itself.

'I can't see anything different,' said Jason.

Chris leaned in through the back door and pushed at the seat. It collapsed suddenly as though it had been balancing precariously in place. In fact, it had. The bolts were on the floor.

'I still don't get it,' I said.

Chris leaned in even farther, pulled away the upright section of seat and poked his arm well into the space behind it, right into the boot. He'd found a way into the boot without opening it with the key!

While Jason and I watched, he bolted both halves of the seat back into place. Good with his hands, Mr Ferguson had said, and that was easy to see (though I could probably think of a few better things he could do with them). By the time he was finished, guess who was also standing beside us. Ben. That's Ben, the invisible man.

'Where the hell did you go?'

He pointed into a garden two houses up from the high paling fence. 'Were my eyes playing tricks, or did that copper really let you put my stash back into the boot?'

'Sure did,' beamed Jason, and the two of them exploded with laughter.

I kicked them both, Jason first because he was my brother and he had known all along what was in that bag, then Ben because it was his stuff and he'd run away and left me to take the rap. Both withdrew strategically to the footpath to see if I would attack again. That left me with Chris Meagher. 'I guess I owe you a big thank you.'

'No. It's all right. Hey, you're one cool chick, I'll give you that. Did you really throw your keys over that fence?'

'I guess I did.'

He whistled in admiration.

I basked in his admiration.

'Look, I was rude to you the other day when you came for petrol. Stared at you like you were some kind of walking centrefold. We don't get many beautiful women around Fergo's.'

Not a bad line. But it wasn't going to work. I'd made a promise to Glenda, hadn't I?

'I hope I've evened up the score a bit.' He nodded towards the boot.

Yes, I thought. You *have* redeemed yourself. Though the petrol station debacle was really my fault, of course, and he didn't have anything to apologise for.

'I'd like to make it up to you even further, if it's all right with you.'

At this moment, the very worst moment he could have chosen, Jason turned up at my shoulder. He must have realised Chris was about to ask me out — but did that stop him? 'Eh, look Rosie, um …'

I turned round quickly and shoved him hard in the chest, making him stagger away. Not very elegant, but hey, I'm a Prestie chick. Then I turned back to face Chris as though nothing had happened.

He was a Prestie too. Didn't even blink. 'We should see a movie together sometime. What do you say?'

No chance. I'd made that promise to Glenda. She was my leash in case I went getting myself into danger. (Woof, woof.)

I looked at Chris — that face, those curls, and the gentle, friendly kind of way he was smiling at me, Rosie Sinclair.

Ah, but there was my promise to Glenda. When you make a promise to your best bud, you should stick to it, eh.

Count to three. Time to make up my mind. Say no, Rosie, say no. Tongue up against the top of the mouth to make an 'N' then lips pushed out in a little 'o'. It felt like Glenda was standing there, coaching me.

But she wasn't there, was she, and what did Glenda know anyway? 'Yeah, OK,' I said.

He didn't look surprised, but I didn't care. My head was spinning. 'I was going to ring you anyway, to apologise,' he said. 'I'll call you tonight. Is that all right?' The arrogance was gone, the teasing smirk of yesterday replaced by a sincerity that reminded me of Todd Rooney. I'd told Glenda that there wasn't enough spark with Todd. Now that Chris was staring down at me, genuinely pleased with what he found, there was more than just a spark. You could have shoved me in a fireplace and toasted marshmallows on my skin.

Jason hadn't gone far away. Now he and Ben ventured off the footpath again. 'Listen, Rosie,' he called. 'We're sorry about all this. But look, it's over now, and we've still got the dope.'

I turned to face them. Yes, I still had the dope, in the boot of my black taxi. I started up the Mercedes while the two guys went round to shake Chris's hand and thank him. Perfect timing.

I planted my foot on the accelerator and took off up the road. Vague shouts of, 'Hey, Rosie, what the hell …!' reached my ears until I was out of range.

I didn't go straight home. There was the question of that black plastic bag to take care of. If I gave it back to Ben he would only get in trouble again, and Jason along with him. Someone had to look out for my braindead brother.

Once I was out of sight I started looking for somewhere to dump the bag. Chris had already mentioned Jimmy Way's, so I couldn't take it there. Ah, just the place. There was an open skip on the footpath in front of a building site. I tossed in the plastic bag and slipped a discarded sheet of plasterboard over the top.

Then I went home wondering how I could keep the truth from Glenda.

FOURTEEN

MR HOSKINS HAD BANNED ME from having the mobile at school, so now I left it in the glove box. Once I had parked the car at home, I decided I had better check my message bank. This was the first message:

Rosie.

A hesitation.

Rosie? Rosie?

Pause.

Oh, you have one of those damn machines. A curse, if you ask me.

Lengthy silence.

Umm, I need a lift ... er, my sister. Oh, I can't think when there's no-one there listening.

Mrs Foat hung up.

This was the second message:

Listen up, girl. I've heard about Paddy and why he's not answering his phone. It makes no difference to me who's driving that black heap of junk. I want the ring. And remember this, too. Your grandfather's in gaol, right? That's a very nasty place to be if you annoy the wrong people. I've got friends in low places, if you get my meaning. Cough up what I'm after, or your grandad's going to have a nasty little accident.

I started to cry, then told myself not to be such a girl. But the voice had threatened Grandad now and he was so vulnerable there in gaol. I saw him in my mind, the way he looked when we had gone to see him last weekend. The prison uniform, the long face. I *had* to find the stupid ring that this horrible man was so eager to get his hands on. It wasn't in the car. Glenda and I had searched it, and I'd had two more goes by myself, even under the bonnet, to see if it was hooked over a spark-plug lead, anything. No sign of it.

If I couldn't find the ring, I had to try and work out who might be making the threats. Glenda had done all she could. There was only one place where I could find out more, distasteful though it was. I had to speak to Uncle Bruce.

After that first call, when I got his answering machine and indulged in a little anonymous abuse, I had called him twice more, leaving a more conventional message with hardly any mention of what a mongrel he was.

122

The mongrel hadn't called back.

There was only one thing for it. I would have to go and find him.

He had a favourite watering hole called Ritt's Hotel. That's right. I haven't got the spelling wrong. A guy named Freddy Ritt had come up with the clever idea of naming a hotel after himself in the hope that people would think it had some connection to a famous swanky place in London called The Ritz. Ha! Some hope. It was the biggest dive in Prestwidge.

I parked the Mercedes under the only light in the car park that hadn't been smashed, crossing my fingers that the light would deter thieves. Better be quick, I told myself. I marched straight in through the front door, making a few heads turn, but no-one challenged me. There was Bruce Larkin, on a stool with his back to me, holding up the bar.

'I want to talk to you,' I announced before he even knew I was behind him.

He hunched his shoulders and put his hands over his head as though he expected to be banged on the noggin. When nothing hit him, he turned around. 'Shit! Rosie. You gave me a fright. What are you doing here?'

'I want to know what's going on. Some ring's gone missing and people think Grandad's got it.'

'Hey, keep your voice down,' he murmured, staring around wildly, but no-one was paying the least attention.

'Don't try to deny it. You were searching for it when I found you in Grandad's car.'

To my surprise, he admitted as much without an argument. 'How did you find out?'

I told him about the sinister phone calls. He let out a worried sigh. 'Word's getting around, then.'

'What's so special about this ring, anyway?'

'What's so special! It's worth twenty thousand dollars, that's what.'

'Shit!' Even I was impressed, not that I gave a damn really. It was Grandad's safety that concerned me. I turned the tables on Bruce. 'So how did you know to look in the Mercedes?'

His head ducked first to one side then to the other before he drew me in close. 'Look, no-one knows for sure. It's all a bit of guesswork, but I've got this mate, right, and he's passed on the word that's doing the rounds. A bloke named McWhirter tried to knock over a jewellery store, going back a few weeks ago. A proper lowlife, really. He never amounted to much in the burglary world, so everyone is surprised he dared to have a go at this place. Anyway, he ended up in hospital.'

'I know about that,' I said. 'He's in a coma.'

'Not any more, he's not.'

That was a surprise. Obviously Bruce's sources were better than Glenda's and mine. 'Well, if he's awake, the police must be onto him with their questions,' I murmured. 'But all the jewellery was recovered, except for this ring that's supposed to be in the Mercedes. Did this McWhirter bloke say he hid it in Grandad's car? Is that what all this fuss is about?'

'No. If he'd told the police that, they would have impounded the car by now. No, the word is, McWhirter can't remember a thing. His brain didn't work so well at the best of times, but now it's like scrambled eggs. That's what the quacks reckon up at the hospital, so McWhirter's not scamming. It's for real.'

'But what's the connection with Grandad's car?'

'I'm only guessing, like I said, but it makes sense to me. Trouble is, it looks like I'm not the only one who's worked it out.'

'What are you talking about? Worked *what* out?'

'The car,' he hissed, doing another check to make sure no-one was listening, but frankly, if there was anyone in the bar who gave two hoots, I couldn't spot them. 'It's because of where Paddy left his car on the night of the robbery.'

'It was outside his mate's place. The one who owned the van.'

'George Goggin,' Bruce reminded me. 'But it's where GG lives that's the point.'

I still didn't have a clue.

'He lives in a little lane off Gresham Street,' Bruce tried to explain, and at last I had a name that made a connection.

'Gresham Street. That's where the jewellery store is!'

'Farr's,' he said, nodding. 'Farr's Fine Jewellery. That's the place McWhirter tried to turn over, only it all went wrong. Someone saw his torch light and rang the cops. Sirens everywhere. He ditched a packet of gemstones on an empty block, but for some reason he wanted a better hiding spot for the ring.'

'Grandad's Mercedes.'

'Ah, *now* you get it. Everyone in Prestwidge knows Paddy Larkin's car, and there it was, parked in the street. McWhirter knows if he's caught with the ring on him he'll end up in gaol, but if he hides it somewhere no-one would think of looking ...'

I beat him to the rest: '... somewhere he can get it back from any time he likes. But doesn't it take time to break into a car?'

Bruce made a rude, dismissive noise through his lips. 'Not if you know what you're doing,' he said, in a tone that showed *he* certainly did. 'That McWhirter was stealing cars before his voice broke. Would have been in and out again in ten seconds flat.'

'So he hides the ring somewhere in the Mercedes and walks off down the street like he's out for a night-time stroll, then gets hit by a drunk on a push-bike. Meanwhile, poor Grandad runs into the police, they search the van and find those parkas, and now *he's* in gaol instead.' (Instead of *you*, I almost added.)

'Dumb bad luck,' said Bruce, as though he were pronouncing fate's verdict from on high.

'But why didn't the police think of all this and come looking for the ring?'

'The police!' he said with disdain. 'They couldn't find their own arseholes with a sniffer dog.'

'So who do you think is making those calls to Grandad's mobile?'

'Could be anyone. Twenty thousand dollars is a lot of money.'

'What's a jewellery store in Prestwidge doing with a ring like that, anyway?'

'Wasn't for sale. Belongs to Terry Sidebottom, or his wife, at least. Engagement ring.'

I'd heard of Mr Sidebottom. His name was always turning up in the local newspaper, along with a picture of his sweating, bloated face. He was a big name in real estate. Everywhere you looked you'd see a sign advertising Prestwidge Land & Housing with his name along the bottom.

'What was it doing in the shop?'

'Being fixed, apparently. That's how they know what it's worth. Terry wanted it valued while it was in for repairs. He's offered a reward, you know. Three thousand dollars. Wants it back for his wife, eh. Sentimental value or something.' He laughed bitterly to himself. 'Sentiment. That's a good one. Terry Sidebottom's a ruthless bastard. Memory or no memory, I wouldn't like to be McWhirter once he gets out of hospital.' This brought a brief chuckle, then the smile disappeared. 'That's what makes these threats on the phone a bit of a worry, Rosie. Everyone knows Sidebottom's reputation. If a bloke's willing to risk getting hold of that ring, considering who it belongs to, then he's sure to be just as ruthless. We're talking about a serious criminal here.'

Suddenly I needed a drink, something to stop my mouth from drying out altogether.

'Rosie,' Bruce said in a whisper, 'you haven't got it, have you?'

I was distracted by my fears for Grandad. 'Got what?'

'The ring, of course.'

I looked at him like he was something stuck on the sole of my shoe. 'Why would I have listened to all this if I already had the damn thing?'

'All right. I was just asking. But if you *did* have it, the best thing would be to give it to me, right?'

Slimeball, I thought to myself. There's his own father in danger of having an "accident" in gaol and he just wants the reward. That's why he asked me. What would that creep on the phone do to Grandad if he found out we'd handed the ring back to the owners? I didn't even want to think about it.

My day ended on a better note, at least. Chris rang after I had been home an hour or so and asked me to the movies on Saturday night. That was fine for a first date; I wouldn't have to meet a lot of his friends at some party where everyone got off their faces. It would be just him and me. Perfect.

FIFTEEN

THE NEXT DAY WAS FRIDAY — and even better than that, it was the last day of term! I honoured a long-standing tradition among Prestwidge Year Twelve students and took the day off. Mental health day, I told myself, and I was serious, too. I had errands for my old people banked up like a freeway at peak hour, and with that threat hanging over Grandad's head, how could I sit in class taking *anything* in? Besides, that dreaded voice had promised to ring back, and this time I had to speak to him, direct. I could hardly sit in the classroom waiting for him to call, could I? Not after Mr Hoskins had declared my mobile *verboten. Sieg Heil!*

I spent the morning catching up on the backlog of short trips around Prestwidge, with the mobile on the front seat beside me. Every time it rang, I jumped. At this rate, I would have an accident soon.

Mrs Foat finally got onto me in person. I picked her up and delivered her to the hospital, and since I had taken care of the other jobs by then, I even went up with her to the third floor to see her sister. She was even further away with the pixies now, poor thing. (I don't want to grow old. I wonder if you can get an exemption, like missing out on PE at school.)

Fortunately Mrs Foat did all the talking. 'It's a lovely day outside, Meredith. My geraniums are doing well. Got to be careful I don't over-water them, though.' Whether her sister took in a single word was hard to tell. After a while, I left them both there and went for a walk. Good for my problem area. Tones it up.

So far there had been no word from the Voice of the Underworld. Did he know I was sweating on his call? Was he following me, watching me become more and more nervous? I looked around, examining every face, near and far. The bastard. Now he'd made me completely paranoid.

It was time to fetch Mrs Foat and take her home when the phone rang. Oh, God. Was it him? What was I going to say?

'Rosie, it's Glenda.'

'Oh, hi!' I let out a relieved sigh.

'Don't you "hi" me, you lying cow.'

Oh, dear. 'Cow' was very high on Glenda's list of unaffectionate terms. I could guess what was coming, but how had she found out?

'What are you on about?' I asked, bluffing shamelessly.

'Don't,' she spluttered. 'Just don't go on with the innocent act, right? You're going out with Chris Meagher after all, aren't you? Don't deny it. I heard it from a girl who buys weed from a halfwit named Ben who's mates with your halfwitted brother.'

I tried to explain how Chris had gallantly rescued me from a life behind bars, but she wouldn't listen. 'I need a lift home from uni, *now*. Come and get me.'

That was a command, not a request. Unfortunately, I couldn't pick Mrs Foat up from the hospital and drive her home without leaving Glenda stranded for an hour. 'Do you mind if I pick up a friend before I take you home?' I asked Mrs Foat when I got back to the hospital.

'Not at all. I'd enjoy a little drive.' She settled into the back seat as though this were a Sunday outing.

She was so quiet and unnoticeable that when I picked up Glenda she didn't even realise my elderly passenger was there. As soon as she had slammed the door shut, she launched into me. 'I warned you, didn't I? You're out of your depth. He's twenty-one years old. Why you don't just go out with Todd Rooney, I can't understand.'

We went over the same ground that we had covered in her bedroom a few days before. Or at least she did. I just listened, wishing I had a half block of mint chocolate. Glenda still hadn't seen Mrs Foat. I glanced over my shoulder and found the old dear staring politely out of the window as though she hadn't heard a word.

Glenda saw me staring and finally turned around. 'Oh, shit!' she exclaimed.

Mrs Foat pretended she hadn't heard all over again while Glenda apologised. I thought it was time I introduced them.

At least this interlude had put a sock in Glenda's mouth. Now I had a chance to respond. 'I tried to explain the other day,' I insisted. 'Todd's a nice boy and does everything sweetly, and he's good-looking and I must say there is a bit of attraction there.' Plus, it makes the girls at school insanely jealous! 'But with Chris, well, I don't know what it is. I want to find out, so I know what it is about him that just makes me feel ...' I shrugged and looked a bit helpless, which wasn't the right thing to do in front of Glenda at that moment.

She craned her neck for another gander at Mrs Foat, who had wound the window down a little to let the breeze play in her wispy grey hair. 'It's sex, isn't it, Rosie?' said Glenda, as softly as she could.

'No, of course not!' I scolded her. I was scandalised. 'Honestly, that's not it at all.' It was the truth — at least I was pretty sure it was. (Bloody hormones!) I had only just met him. Barely spoken to him, really and I wasn't that kind of girl, as Glenda knew only too well, being my best friend.

She gave me that older sister look. 'Look, this is the classic dilemma and you're hardly the first girl who's been there. Nice boy versus dangerous brute. You're attracted to Chris because he's someone you know you shouldn't go anywhere near.'

'What, a couple of semesters of psychology and you know all about it, do you?'

'This is nothing to do with psychology. This is real life. You can still call off the date, you know.'

'No, I can't do that. I'd be too embarrassed.'

'No problem. I'll ring him for you. I'll tell him you're washing your hair or something.'

'Don't you dare. Oh, Glenda, do you really think he's no good for me?'

'YES,' she said with a Paddy Larkin firmness that unnerved me. I stopped arguing so that she would stop trying to convince me. I was sort of half convinced she was right, even though I didn't want to be. Oh God, what should I do?

Glenda needed a few things at The Grove. 'I'll take Mrs Foat home then come back for you.'

She waved as she got out. That left just Mrs Foat and me in the car. 'I'm sorry about all these detours,' I said.

'Not at all, Rosie. I've quite enjoyed myself.'

From her tone, I suspected she wasn't just talking about the ride. 'I hope we didn't shock you with all that girl-talk.'

'Shock me? Oh, goodness, no. I must confess to you, Rosie, I listened to every word.'

She was smiling openly now. 'You two are just like me and my girlfriends from years ago. Good to see you modern ones still talk about the same things. I was worried the hairy-legged crowd and the bra burners had banished all that liveliness out of you young things.'

I wasn't sure who she was talking about. I wasn't into shaving my legs too often myself, but that stuff about bras sounded decidedly off.

'You never forget, you know,' she said whimsically, still with the wind in her hair. 'For me, it was a boy named Colin. Oh, he was a wild one. I used to go weak at the knees every time I saw him. He noticed me, too, I made sure of that.' She latched onto some memory that sent her cheeks a healthy pink. Then she leaned forward on the seat and urged in a half-whisper, 'Don't let your friend talk you out of it, Rosie. There's plenty of time to be safe, and it's a long life to live without a bit of passion to remember on those lonely nights.'

I remembered the photos I'd seen in her house. 'Your husband,' I said, cautiously, 'his name wasn't Colin, was it?'

'No, dear. It was Geoffrey.'

We rode on in silence for almost a minute and then, 'Go for the dangerous one, girl,' she said, like I was a horse and she'd backed me in the Melbourne Cup.

And that's how it happened that Mrs Foat of all people helped me to make up my mind.

I went back to get Glenda and took her home as well, though I didn't go inside. When I arrived back at my place, the creature on the sofa showed signs of life and eventually spoke. The shock nearly bowled me over. 'There was a call for you,' he announced listlessly. 'Some guy. Number's on the pad beside the phone.'

At last Jason had found useful employment. He was an answering machine.

'Did he say his name?'

'Yeah.'

Silence followed. I'd better retract that last statement about my brother. At least an answering machine would repeat the full message, and usually you could at least tell who it was from the sound of the voice.

'Well?'

'I'm thinking.'

I wondered what the strange noise was.

'Was it Chris?'

'No,' he said uncertainly. 'Ted, or something like that.'

'Todd.'

'Yeah, that was it.' Jason found a half-finished biscuit among the blankets, which seemed to please him. Now he wouldn't have to go to the kitchen for something to eat.

I took the cordless phone into my bedroom and rang Todd Rooney.

'Oh, hi, Rosie. Thanks for calling back,' he said.

'Sorry I wasn't here when you called.'

'No worries,' he said cheerfully. 'I tried to get you a couple of times last week, but you're hardly ever at home. Have you got a mobile?'

'It's not working,' I lied. 'There's something wrong with the battery and I have to keep it turned off a lot of the time.'

He didn't seem to mind. In fact, he started talking as though it were only yesterday that we'd been to that party. He was so easy to listen to, and I just lay back on the bed, laughing at some of the things he said about his parents. He was a nice guy, no doubt about that.

Then he came to the point. 'Listen, Rosie. We had a great night when we went out. Want to do it again some time?'

'Yeah, sure,' I said before I'd thought about it.

'Cool.' I could just see his smile at the other end of the line. 'I was thinking of tomorrow night, actually. Just you and me this time.'

Tomorrow night! Think quickly. I realised suddenly that despite everything I had said to Glenda, I would quite like to go out with Todd again. But tomorrow night I was going to the movies with Chris Meagher, and I wasn't about to break my date with him. (It wasn't just me now. I had to keep faith with Mrs Foat, didn't I?)

136

I was very careful about the next sounds I made, trying for that perfect mixture of disappointment and regret. 'Oh, Todd, I'm sorry. I can't. Not tomorrow night.' *Insert excuse here.* But *what* excuse? I hadn't thought of one yet. There was no time to work on different options. My tongue just kept moving, hoping that my brain would send down the signal in time.

'I've got to baby-sit.' Phew! Give yourself a high five, girl! 'I can't get out of it, either. The lady booked it up a week ago and she rang me again just now to confirm, so I can't let her down.'

He sounded heartbroken, but took it well. 'I'll organise something else, then. Another night.'

'Yes. I'd like that.' We talked on a bit more, and then he had to go, still sounding disappointed. I took the phone back to its base on the kitchen wall. 'Rosie Sinclair,' I said out loud, making sure Jason couldn't hear me, 'you want to have your cake and eat it too.'

Cake is for wimps. I needed chocolate.

Mum was home by this time. 'We're out of milk,' I lied. 'I'd better go up to the corner store and get some. Can I have some money?' This was an old scam I'd learned in primary school as a way of supplementing my limited supplies of cash. Mum couldn't be bothered handing out coins from her purse and always gave me a note instead. Never remembered to ask for the change. This time she handed over a ten-dollar note.

At the store I got the milk out of the way first then went looking for the chocolate. Actually, I could hear it calling to me from three aisles away, 'Rosie, Rosie', and there it was, the strongest calls coming from a large block with soft mint centres.

No, I told myself severely, a whole family-sized block would be indulgent, an absolute extravagance, even if I had the money, which I did. Not to mention what it would do to my problem area. But this was a major drama I had to get over, here. Two-timing boys was not something I had ever done before. Then there was the stuff that Glenda wouldn't tell me about from her relationship with Chris a couple of years ago, and I hadn't even dared think about that yet.

What the heck. I bought the largest size and ate two rows in the car on the way home. The guilt became unbearable, which meant I needed someone to tell me off. Glenda seemed the best choice, and I knew she wouldn't have turned into Giselle just yet.

I phoned her as soon as I reached home. She didn't have to know about all the lies I'd told, of course. It wasn't confession, for God's sake. I told her just enough so she could keep up her end of the conversation.

'You turned down a date with *Todd Rooney*? That's a crime,' she exploded down the line at me. 'Listen, girlfriend, those hormones of yours will end up with a criminal record.' She scolded me for another five minutes, then stopped abruptly. 'What's that smacking sound?'

'What sound?'

'In my ear. It's been going on ever since you called me. You're eating something.'

'No.'

'Don't lie to me, Rosie. It's chocolate. Mint centres. I can smell it from here.'

'Glenda, we're on the phone.'

'Doesn't matter. I know you. What size block did you get?'

'The smallest one. Snack size.'

'It's a big block, isn't it?'

'No.'

'How much is left?'

I looked down at the silver wrapping paper. 'Not a lot.'

'You're hopeless, honestly. Save the rest for me.'

I did. (Well, I saved her the last row.)

SIXTEEN

On Saturday, all the old people of Prestwidge must have found someone else to be their taxi, because they left me alone all day to worry about my date with Chris Meagher.

The eternal question: what to wear? In the circumstances, my access to Glenda's wardrobe seemed cut off for the time being, and the one thing of hers that I did have, the little black skirt, was attached to that scene at the servo which I'd rather forget. Nothing in my wardrobe. Time to shop.

There was a fabulous skirt in Rags for Ragers that I'd had my eye on for weeks. It was red, with gold embroidery just above the hem. I'd tried it on so many times the sale assistant couldn't even be bothered getting her hopes up when I turned up yet again to check it out. Way too expensive, of course. It would empty my humble bank account completely, but without Glenda along to act as my good sense, I bought it anyway.

And now, the top … what top could possibly match my new skirt? No chance of buying a new one. I went through my wardrobe. Flick, no; flick, no; flick, can't wear pink with red. There was a nice white one, but it had tacky silvery spangles dusted over the bust. *So* passé. God, what was I thinking when I bought it? On I went. Flick, no; flick, no; flick, STOP. There it was. Black would go perfectly with my new skirt. But the neckline! Somehow I had found the courage to buy it, but I had never dared wear it.

I took it off the hanger. (Thank God for hormones.) If the A List could see me now they would put blindfolds on their boyfriends, then beg me for fashion tips. For a few moments I indulged in this pleasing fantasy. No, I decided, I don't need Justine's or Clare's or Fiona's approval. Plunging neckline or not, Rosie was still Rosie.

He had said seven o'clock. At seven-thirty there was still no sign of him. Glenda has a rule. If they are more than twenty minutes late, the date is off, which just goes to show she has never been desperate to go out with any one guy. But he might have had the courtesy to ring and say he would be late. Frown, grumble. I tried watching some mindless TV with the resident zombie for a while to distract me. I had to keep turning away every time Mum walked into the room in case she saw my top and chucked a mental.

At a quarter to eight a car finally pulled up outside, and I hurried out the front door and down the path so he wouldn't have to come in and see Jason on the couch, or worse, meet my mother. I was a bit disappointed to see that the car was actually a ute, the same one Chris had been driving when he rescued me from Constable Enright. It sported mag wheels and a fox's tail on the tip of the aerial. A typical Prestiemobile. What the hell, I'm a typical Prestie chick.

He climbed out of the car and watched me pick my way through the cracked concrete of our front path in my ridiculously high heels. 'Hi!' he called brightly as he walked round to the curb. No apology for being forty-five minutes late. 'Hey, you look great.'

I forgot about apologies. Every cent I'd spent on the skirt had been worth it, and so had the hour and twenty minutes I'd spent in front of the mirror getting my make-up right. Chris opened the door for me and I slipped into the seat. At least I tried to. My bottom just kept going down until it couldn't go any further. The halt was rather sudden. More than that, it was painful. 'Ouch!' I cried.

I pulled myself up quickly and heard an ominous rip. 'Oh, shit, no,' I swore, which wasn't very ladylike but even the Queen of England would have said something rude if she'd heard that sound. 'My skirt!'

I was out on the footpath again by now, contorting my body like a dog trying to catch its tail so I could see what had happened to my brand-new skirt. In the end, I had to loosen it at the waist and turn it round ninety degrees which isn't something you do in front of a boy on the first date if you can avoid it. There it was, a rip in the material.

'Not too big,' said Chris soothingly.

'*Not too big!*' I repeated, keeping my voice to a low shout. 'It might as well be a metre wide.' In fact, it was closer to a centimetre, but the skirt was still ruined.

'Must be a spring. This is Darren's ute and hardly anyone sits in that seat. Just his dog, mainly.'

'Oh, thanks. That makes me feel much better. Where's *your* car?'

'Still up on the hoist at Fergo's. That's why I'm late. Couldn't get the new muffler fitted in time.'

Still no apology, but at least there was an excuse. I angrily straightened my skirt. 'Damn! I just got this from Rags for Ragers this morning.'

'Don't worry about it,' he said, as though I were making a fuss about nothing. 'I'll get something to put over the spring.'

While I tossed up whether to go back inside and change, he threw back the tarpaulin that covered the back of Darren's ute and rummaged around in the darkness. I decided to stay put, mainly because there was nothing in my wardrobe that looked half decent, and besides, if I went back inside now Mum would want to know why, and it would all be a hundred times more embarrassing than it already was. *Not a good start.*

It didn't get any better when Chris pulled out a piece of cardboard. 'Here, this should do the trick.'

'I can't sit on that. It's filthy.'

He looked at it more closely. 'Yeah, s'pose it is.' He went back to looking.

'I've got a better idea. We can go in the Mercedes.'

He stopped his hopeful fossicking about under the tarp and stood looking at me.

'Yeah, all right,' he answered, not needing to be persuaded. 'I love those old cars. So well built.'

Just like you are, I thought to myself. We walked to the car, both of us arriving at the driver's door together. He had his hand out for the keys.

'Sorry, Chris. This is my grandad's car. I can't let anyone else drive it. It was a promise I made to him.'

Technically this was a lie. It was only certain members of the family who were disqualified like Uncle Bruce and Mum and Jason and Grandma — *all* the family, come to think of it — but I wasn't giving up those keys to Chris either.

'Come on, Rosie. Girls don't drive. It's the guy's job, especially when I'm taking you out.'

I made a face that said there was nothing I could do about it. He sighed and walked round to the door on the passenger's side, climbed in and folded his arms rather sullenly. This wasn't going the way either of us had planned.

It got worse.

I drove out onto Hedges Avenue then turned into The Promenade, which swept grandly down to the white-box monstrosity of Prestwidge Grove. The Promenade is a dual carriageway, with two lanes in each direction. I was cruising just on the speed limit when a car swept up beside us, in a hurry to get somewhere. It was a big, ugly sedan that made the same deep rumbling noise I had heard coming from Darren's ute. Chris turned instinctively to look at it.

'Oh, great,' he sighed when he saw the occupants. Typical Presties, with mullet haircuts and flannies. These two guys also wore sunglasses and a look like they had been chiselled out of rock. The passenger had his window down and his arm resting halfway out the door. 'Hey, Meagher. That's you, isn't it? Lost your licence, have you, mate?'

Chris ignored them, but I could see he wasn't happy.

'Just as well you've got a sheila to do the driving for you then, eh?'

I rolled up the window, but by then they had lost interest anyway. The driver put the pedal to the metal and they roared off.

My dream date didn't say a word. I thought it best to do the same. Maybe we should have turned around, gone home, started all over again, pretended my skirt wasn't ripped. Maybe I should even have let him drive Grandad's car. We didn't do any of these things, hoping it would all somehow get better, but sometimes the planets are just aligned the wrong way in the sky.

As I stood beside Chris in the queue to buy our tickets, I saw a face staring at me. It was Todd Rooney.

He came over. 'Hi, Rosie,' he said, with a look on his face I couldn't read. 'This is the baby you had to mind, is it?'

I deserved that.

Chris didn't know what was going on, but he sensed the sarcasm in Todd's voice. 'Hey, sonny boy. Watch the way you talk to Rosie or I'll rearrange your pretty face.'

That would have been just perfect, a fight between Todd and Chris, but Todd wasn't interested in a punch-up and he knew he would get pummelled anyway. He backed away to join his mates.

Chris and I sat through the movie, separately, like two people who didn't know each other.

'Do you want to go for coffee?' he asked me afterwards.

I could tell from the tone of his voice that he was hoping I'd say no.

'Sorry, I'm tired.'

I drove home. On the footpath beside Darren's ute we stood together, not daring to look at each other. 'I'm really sorry, Rosie. I was looking forward to tonight. You're very pretty, you know.' Then he leaned across and pecked me on the cheek. 'Goodnight.'

What a disaster. Could it have been any worse? I went into my bedroom and just lay there in the dark with my hand to my face. I was touching the skin of my cheek where he'd kissed me, ever so lightly. Despite everything, it burned.

How could it have all gone so wrong, so quickly? I was thinking. I know he likes me. There's a kind of light in his eyes when he looks at me. It was there when he first turned up tonight, and I swear I could see it again when he told me how pretty I was and gave me that peck on the cheek. So what happened in between? He did wreck my skirt, and who wouldn't be a bit upset about that?

Some guys are hard work.

I wished I could talk to Glenda about it. There was my bag on the edge of the bed, with the mobile inside. I fished it out, but there was no point. She was being Giselle tonight and wouldn't get home until about five in the morning. She needed to sleep when she did make it home, so I couldn't ring until tomorrow afternoon. Even if I could catch her between shows at the club, I was in for a huge slice of 'I told you so.'

My room was dark and cold and lonely, just like my mood. I couldn't be bothered getting undressed, so I simply pulled a blanket over myself and kicked my shoes out from under it. They landed with a heavy thud, one then the other, on the floor. Sounded like my heart sinking. Come on sleep, I thought, make it all go away.

As soon as I started to drift off, a new worry crept into my head. How was I going to get petrol for the Merc without seeing Chris? I drifted into half-sleep again. Then a phone started ringing far away. I wished Mum would answer it, because it was keeping me back from that last step down the ladder into deep sleep. Come on, Mum, answer it. It was a familiar ring, one that I just couldn't ignore. Like Grandad's mobile. Yeah, a bit like that. Silly tune.

It *was* Grandad's mobile! I wrenched myself quickly out of sleep. Where was it? The sound was muffled, because the phone had become tangled in the bedclothes. At last I found it and felt for the big Answer button, hoping despite myself that I would hear Glenda's voice when I put it to my ear.

'Are you ready to hand over that ring yet, girlie?' said a voice that was becoming all too familiar.

It was the 'girlie' part that did it. If he had just said 'girl' I might have stayed calm. But 'girlie'? Who did he think he was? I was fed up with this rude mongrel and I told him so. 'I'm fed up with you, you rude mongrel,' I shouted into the phone. For a few seconds it didn't matter who he was or what he wanted, I went for him. All the fear and the frustration and the tension I'd felt in my shoulders these last few days was because of him. 'Look, buster,' I said bluntly, 'I'm sick of you ringing me up at whatever time it suits you, making threats about my grandad. I haven't got the stupid ring from that robbery. Do you understand that? NOT-HERE. SOME-WHERE-ELSE. Do I have to draw you a map? It's not in the car. I've been over it from one end to the other five times.'

Wow, I even surprised myself. To tell you the truth, I think the failure of my dream date with Chris might have had something to do with it. Whatever … I wasn't finished yet. Before he could speak, I was at him again. 'I'm sick of hearing about that ring, do you hear me? I don't care what it's worth or whether there's a reward or if you're some big-time criminal. You know what I'd do if I did have it? I wouldn't give it to you, that's for sure. I'd … I'd take it to the police.'

There was an odd silence. I don't know quite what I expected, but was that a sudden intake of breath I heard coming down the line? In each of the calls I'd had from this horrible man he had lorded it over me completely, yet here was a moment of vulnerability that I couldn't understand. What had I said?

But it seems I had misread that silence badly. He was just gathering himself to return my anger with interest. 'Now, you listen to me. If you're one of Larkin's brood then you're no doubt a thief like him. You're holding out on me, going right to the edge same as any thief would, hoping I'll just go away and you can have that ring for yourself. Well, it won't work with me, understand? I want that ring in *my* hands and no-one else's. If you take it anywhere near the police, it's Paddy who'll pay the price. Do you understand me? Maybe I should make it a bit clearer. Have you seen the heavy doors they've got in that gaol? Very dangerous, those doors. You have to watch where you put your hands, especially round the hinges. People have been know to lose a finger or two in those doors.'

I cringed at the thought. I couldn't help it. I even bent my own fingers, opening and closing them over my palm in reaction. 'Please …' I whimpered pathetically.

It was what he wanted to hear, I think, because he eased up and became more businesslike. 'I'll call again and make arrangements to get the ring, and if by any chance you're telling the truth and you haven't found it yet, you'd better get looking. Remember, as soon as that ring is in my hands, your grandad's suddenly a very safe man.'

SEVENTEEN

ON SUNDAY MORNING, I HAD a long-standing engagement. Normally, when my old people needed to go somewhere, they rang up and expected me to be there straightaway, like I was a taxi. But this gig was arranged days beforehand. Mrs Duval was going to bingo.

It was Mr Duval who rang me on Friday, just to make sure I hadn't forgotten. I'd heard about how old people have their little rituals and if they get disrupted it can upset them for days afterwards. I assured the dear old thing that I wouldn't let his wife down.

So, after a night spent worrying about Grandad, the hole in my skirt and most of all the huge hole in my heart, I pulled up outside the Duvals' house at a few minutes to ten. They welcomed me like I was *their* granddaughter, not Paddy's. Janice was well dressed for the occasion, in a soft pastel twin-set and pleated skirt. 'Those heels are a bit high,' I commented, then bit my tongue. For a second I'd sounded like my mother — 'You can't go out in that.' All the same, I was surprised. I mean, Mrs D sometimes needed a hand on the stairs, and though these shoes only had heels an inch high, if she went over in them she'd break her ankle for sure. But then, bingo is a big thing with some people, I gather, and most of the players would be old dears like herself. It was her big chance to get out the gladrags and show off a bit.

Eric was bustling about making sure she had everything: her purse to buy cards, the cinnamon cake she had made yesterday especially for this occasion. He was putting plastic wrap over it as I came in. I thought to myself, I bet he enjoys this little interlude each month. The only time he has the house to himself. I wonder, does he put his feet on the furniture, sit round with his shirt off in front of the TV, drinking beer straight from the bottle and burping like a yobbo? They had an ancient stereo, with a turntable instead of a CD player. Maybe he cranks it up and plays Frank Sinatra records at full volume. Wow. Boogie time for wrinklies. What a thought.

Mrs Duval was ready to go. 'Where is this bingo hall?' I asked as I was helping her into the Mercedes.

'Downstairs at the RSL,' she said.

Now, I know the RSL pretty well, because it's Grandad's favourite watering hole and the only thing downstairs at the RSL is a car park. I pointed this out.

'Not Prestwidge, dear. The Martindale RSL.'

'Martindale? That's a long way just to play bingo.'

'I have old friends there,' she responded. 'It's how we stay in touch.'

Fine with me. She had too many old friends out at the cemetery for me to complain. I aimed the Merc towards Martindale. Maplethorpe Road was the best way, I decided, almost a freeway at this time on a Sunday morning, but as soon as I turned onto it, I noticed Mrs D shift in her seat, as though she were about to say something. She was watching me closely.

'Rosie,' she said finally, 'has Paddy said anything to you about my bingo?'

I shook my head. 'I don't get much of a chance to see him, do I?'

'No, of course not. I didn't mean to be insensitive.' She fell silent again while the Mercedes ate up another kilometre's worth of fuel.

'Actually, Rosie,' she said suddenly, 'could you turn left at those lights up ahead?'

'But Martingale's straight on …'

'I've changed my mind,' she said. 'I might miss bingo for this week. There's a friend of mine who's not well. Perhaps I should pay them a visit instead.'

This was something of a shock after all the enthusiasm for bingo. I turned left as she commanded and, soon afterwards right into Hedges Avenue. So I wasn't destined to escape Prestwidge that day, after all. She was becoming excited now, shifting constantly in her seat and keen to show me where to turn off the main road. In fact, she was downright jittery as she guided me through a few more side streets.

'Is your friend very ill?' I asked. I had Mrs Foat's sister in mind and wondered whether it would be a bedside vigil for Janice as well.

She didn't answer. She was concentrating too hard on finding the street. 'Here,' she said excitedly. 'The green house just a few doors along.'

I pulled into the curb and cut the engine.

'I can manage from here, thank you, Rosie,' said Mrs Duval. 'You stay in the car.'

'Are you sure?' I asked, concerned.

'Yes, perfectly sure. Now, you'll be back for me at three, won't you?'

I nodded. That was the arrangement, and once I'd dropped her home again I would go round to Glenda's and let her talk me out of becoming a nun.

'Oh, here. Don't forget your cinnamon cake,' I reminded her, holding it out to her.

'You have it, dear,' she said, barely turning her head, as though she couldn't care less about it. 'It's really your grandfather who likes cinnamon cake.'

Well, I knew that, but …

This was all a bit strange. I watched as Mrs Duval worked her way out of the Mercedes, and only then did I look up at the house. There was a man standing on the porch, watching her come along the path. Somehow, I had assumed it was a woman she would be visiting. Wait a minute, I thought. I know that stance, that look. There's no surprise here. This old bloke is expecting her! But how could he have known Mrs Duval was coming when she herself only changed her mind ten minutes ago? There was something suspicious happening here. If she knew she was going to meet a sick friend, why all that pretence back at the house about the bingo?

I watched Mrs Duval walk along the garden path, beginning to think that *I* was being led along a garden path myself. In the time I'd known her I'd never seen her walk with as much enthusiasm.

The man came down the three steps from the porch, as though he wanted to take her arm and help her into the house. He took more than her arm. He had his arm around her shoulder as they mounted the steps, then, in the last couple of strides before they disappeared through the door, his arm dropped affectionately to her waist.

The penny finally dropped. I knew what was going on here! At last I'd found out why Grandad had wanted me to be discreet. Bingo! Ha! Dear old Mrs Duval had a boyfriend!

Poor Eric, I thought as I drove back along Hedges Avenue. The whole thing had been such a shock that I'd had to stop somewhere for a coffee and a think. *Discreet*? I was *speechless*! Now I was back in the car, heading for home. The mobile rang, making me jump. It wouldn't be that horrible man again, surely.

'Hello?'

'Rosie? It's Eric Duval.'

Here was my first chance to practise being discreet. 'Oh, hi, Mr Duval. Is anything the matter?' Butter wouldn't melt in my mouth.

'No, just ringing to see if you got Janice to her bingo all right.'

'Yeah, no problem.' I cringed.

'Oh, that's good, then.' Brief pause. 'Listen, Rosie. I wonder, could I impose upon you again, just for a short trip this time? It's really rather important.'

I felt so sorry for the guy I would have driven him right across the country if he had asked. I turned off towards the Duval house for the second time that morning. Eric was waiting for me, better dressed now, with his hair done neatly and his leather shoes shining. I wondered whether Mrs D even noticed when he got dressed up these days.

'Where to?'

'Oh, a friend of mine rang to ask me over for a drink. I'll show you the way.'

He had mentioned that this trip was important, and I somehow didn't think a drink with an old mate fell quite into that category. But what the heck. He needed a bit of sympathetic handling, even if he didn't realise it.

'Just head onto Hedges Avenue to start with,' he told me. I was very conscious of how I had been on this road already this morning when by right I shouldn't have been, and of how discretion meant I couldn't give myself away by saying so. Then Eric pointed to a corner ahead. 'Turn up there, if you would.'

It was the same place I'd turned off for Mrs Duval. Just a coincidence, I decided. There was a lot of Prestwidge we could be going to yet. My confidence started to slip mightily, though, when he gave me the next direction. We were definitely following the same route, and if we kept on like this we would end up outside that little green house. Butterflies did disgusting things in my stomach. Did he know? Was he making me drive him to that same house to confront the lovers? I couldn't bear to think of the scene that would follow. We were no more than a few streets away now. I considered faking a problem with the Merc, but I didn't know the first thing about engines and he would probably see though my silly pretence in a matter of seconds.

Here was the road coming up. If he told me to turn here, I would know for sure.

He didn't. He stayed silent, and I calmed down enough to realise he was as excited and jumpy in his seat as his wife had been half an hour earlier. What was going on here?

I kept following the road, which was long for a suburban street. Finally, a turn to the left and another to the right. 'Number seventeen,' he said. We were a good half kilometre from the green house and

Mrs Duval. It's all a coincidence, I told myself. His drinking mate just happens to live close by. Crisis over.

Whoever owned number seventeen was a keen gardener. There was a line of magnificent crimson roses just inside the white picket fence, and near the gate a riot of colour from four or five plants I didn't recognise. 'Could you come for me about two o'clock, Rosie? I'd like to be home when Janice gets back from bingo.'

Oh, you poor man, I thought to myself. Your wife seems like such a charmer, Eric, but she's cheating on you! Be discreet, I told myself over and over again. It would probably hurt her as much as him if I gave the game away.

I looked at the house. A curtain was pushed aside at the bottom and a face appeared briefly before it fell into place again. I didn't see much of that face, but enough to know it was a woman's. The mate's wife, I supposed.

Eric was out of the car and waving me off happily and I was in no mood to hang around in case I was indiscreet somehow. The Mercedes purred its way to the end of the road, but the quickest way home was to hang a U-turn at the end of the street and go back the way I had come. I cruised past number seventeen again and there was Eric still outside the gate. He had stopped to pick a posy of flowers from among those colourful blooms I had spotted earlier. He put them behind his back and headed for the front door. There was something about the way he walked up the path. Where had I seen that same walk recently? Then it hit me. His own wife, the cheating Janice, had had the same spring in *her* step.

The door of the little white house opened, and there was the woman I had glimpsed in the window. Where was the husband, the man Eric had come to have a drink with? Come to think of it, where was Eric's beer? If you went round to a friend's house to crack open a few cold ones, you usually took some with you. But not Eric. He was arriving with a bunch of flowers, which he gave to the grey-haired lady in the doorway.

I was almost past the house now, and if I didn't turn my eyes back to the road I'd probably run into something, but I held on just that extra second. It was in that second that I saw it. That woman, grey haired or not, threw her arms eagerly around Eric Duval's neck and kissed him square on the mouth.

Rosie Sinclair! What have you stumbled upon? They were *both* at it! I would have to reassess my view of the aged. Maybe it's not all false teeth and rocking chairs. Maybe retirement just means more time for mischief.

And they've got the gall to complain about young people!

EIGHTEEN

'I'M DISGUSTED,' SAID GLENDA.

I was back in her bedroom, one leg folded under me as I sat on the end of her bed. She might have been talking about my date with Chris Meagher but she wasn't. I had just told her about the Duvals.

'Those randy old devils. The pair of them!' She thought about it for a moment. 'I hope I'm like that when I'm old.' Then she laughed out loud. 'Brings a whole new meaning to the word "bingo".' Yes, well … the less said about that the better.

The smile stayed on her face while I told her about my terrible night with Chris. There was no 'I told you so'. In fact, she seemed downright relieved.

'Good,' she said when I told her how I had lain on my bed afterwards wrapped up in my own misery. 'That's the end of that, thank God. You *are* over this stupid crush, aren't you?'

'*Crush?* That's insulting. Thirteen-year-olds have crushes. This was more of a *rush*.'

'Yeah, a rush of blood to your head — or some other parts of your body, more likely. You *should* become a nun after all. Wouldn't need a leash on your hormones then.'

I had mentioned the nun bit in my report of last night. It's a hard call when your best bud wants to pack you off to a convent. I reminded her that she was the one who took her clothes off in front of pathetic middle-aged men in smoky rooms and she cooled down a bit after that. 'But you've definitely given up on Meagher, right?'

'Yes, definitely,' I conceded. I sort of believed it myself. Anyway, the look I gave her must have been convincing. We went for a coffee in The Grove, which was the only place open in cosmopolitan Prestwidge on a Sunday afternoon. I had the mobile with me, but it was switched off now, and I didn't dare turn it back on in case Mr Underworld wanted to make arrangements for the handover of that missing ring. How was I going to convince him that it simply wasn't there?

Monday. Not my favourite day of the week during school term, but this was the holidays and so

Monday sounded like the beginning of something exciting. I stayed in bed while Mum went off to the salon as usual. The mobile stayed off to make sure I didn't find myself talking to you-know-who, but that didn't stop Mrs Duval. She rang on our home phone.

'I need to make an appointment at the hairdresser's,' she told me. 'If it's not too much trouble, Rosie, what time can you pick me up?'

'Are you going to Hair by Sinclair?' I asked. 'Mum gives a discount to pensioners on Mondays.'

'I know, dear.'

Of course she'd know. Half the old things in Prestwidge had their hair defiled at Hair by Sinclair on a Monday because of that discount. Maybe my mother wasn't really as stupid as she acted most of the time. Mid-morning I set out to pick up Mrs Duval, who had lost all her charm as far as I was concerned. It was as much as I could do to stop myself from asking about her boyfriend. (Discretion, discretion.) Maybe he had said something uncomplimentary about her hair and that was why she wanted to change it. Purple foils, maybe, to go with her rager's image.

Oh, shut up, Rosie, I told myself. You're just jealous because Mrs Duval has more romance in her life than you have.

That hurt.

During uni holidays Glenda sometimes earned extra money at the salon, and if bookings weren't heavy Mum or Tracey would take the day off. Tracey was away, and Glenda was there when I arrived with

Mrs D. There wasn't much point in my taking off somewhere else when I would have to come back for Janice anyway, so I hung around for a chat.

Glenda ticked off the name 'Duval' in the appointments book then made a face at me. I didn't like the look of that expression. Far too mischievous for my liking. She clipped the apron around the old woman's neck and asked, 'How was the bingo yesterday?'

The magazine I had just picked up flopped noisily to the floor. They both turned to look at me as though I were a clumsy idiot, but at the same time I could see that Mrs Duval was searching my face apprehensively. 'Er, I didn't actually go yesterday,' she said. 'Visited a sick friend instead, didn't I, Rosie?'

'There's always next time,' said Glenda innocently. 'You must enjoy it, then.'

'What's that?' asked Mrs Duval absently.

'Bingo.'

'Oh yes, I *do* enjoy it.'

'I'll bet you do. Do you go often?'

'Once a month. It's as much as I can manage.'

'Right,' said Glenda, winking at me over the woman's head.

The conversation went on like this, back and forth for a minute or two, as meaningless as anything said in that salon every Monday morning yet in others ways too salacious for me to repeat. Glenda ended up cutting herself with the scissors while stifling her giggles. Poetic justice. Personally, I was mortified, especially when another woman who had come in for a perm joined in. 'My husband likes bingo. He'd go three times a week if I let him. If *I* can't go, he takes his dog with him.'

There was a desperate gurgling sound from Glenda, who had to excuse herself, pretending she needed the toilet, but I could hear her raucous laughter coming from the little back room. I just hoped the woman didn't work it out. Mum didn't have a clue what was going on, or maybe she thought Glenda was crying, because she told the old duck, 'Boyfriend trouble most likely.'

'I'll tell you something I heard at bingo last time I was there,' said Mrs Duval while Glenda was still absent, desperately trying to compose herself. 'I heard there's a reward being offered for a missing ring.'

Bingo nothing. She must have heard it from her lover. Anyway, she was well informed. My ears stood to attention. 'It's that Terry Sidebottom. He's offering three thousand dollars for the return of his wife's engagement ring.'

'*The* engagement ring!' Mum exploded. 'You mean the massive rock she's been flashing around for years? It's been *stolen*?'

'Yes. Apparently it was taken from Farr's up there on Gresham Street while it was in having one of the claws fixed.'

'It'd need claws like a giant crab to keep that diamond in place. How'd it get damaged?'

Janice didn't know, but the beauty of Hair by Sinclair was that gaps in the gossip could usually be filled in by someone else. In this case it was the woman whose husband liked to play bingo with his dog. I had seen her before, in my sad days as an apprentice. Veronica someone. At that moment she was leaning backwards while her hair was rinsed in the basin, but she could have had her ears six inches underwater and she would still have heard every word, I guarantee it.

'Jammed in a car door, that's what I heard. Mrs Sidebottom was having lunch with some friends at that posh new restaurant on Gresham Street. Too much of a tipple, if you get my meaning.' Even tipped over on her back like a beached turtle, she casually mimicked the universal sign for a drunk bending the elbow. 'She was lucky she didn't lose the stone altogether. Just broke two of the gold claws.'

This led to a lot of breathless and envious discussion about the dangers of pretentious rings that sit too high off the fingers and are always being jagged on things.

'I remember when the lovely Narelle first got that ring,' said Mum excitedly. 'That must be twelve, no, more like fifteen years ago. Heavens, the scandal.'

'Scandal? What are you talking about?' I asked cautiously.

'The Sidebottoms, of course,' Mum informed me, as though I should know. It was a minor detail that I had barely been out of nappies back then. 'The lovely Narelle's not his first wife.' She turned to Veronica, who confirmed her story with a knowing smirk. 'He'd married that girl he got pregnant straight after school, remember?' There was a collective nodding of heads. 'Poor thing. Stuck at home with the baby while Terry chased after every skirt in Prestwidge. He made eyes at me once, you know.'

Glenda had just returned from the bathroom, but on hearing this she stopped dead in her tracks. Mrs Duval turned round in her chair. I looked up from my magazine. Even Veronica had to stare at her, which was unfortunate, since she was still dripping wet and the water ran right down her back.

The sudden silence and this open-mouthed staring discomforted my mother a little. 'He was drunk at the time, of course.'

Ah, that explained it. We all went back to what we were doing.

The conversation might have ended there if I had let it, but here was the best source of information about the ring I was likely to find. 'This ring is a bit special, you say?'

'*Special!*' the three women chorused.

'It's a legend around Prestwidge,' Mum explained. 'It was only when he came up with the ring that the lovely Narelle agreed to marry him. Don't know why he wanted her. Good-looking maybe, but most blokes were scared of her even then. These days she's an absolute dragon.'

'But he was married already!'

'Didn't mean anything to him, did it? I doubt it meant much to the lovely Narelle, either. She was more concerned about his money ...'

'*And* where he got it from,' added Veronica sagely.

'What was wrong with his money?' I asked naively. I had visions of a woman sniffing fifty-dollar notes to see if they reeked of garlic.

'He was a crook. As big as they get around Prestwidge. The police couldn't touch him, could they? Too clever. But Narelle knew his luck would run out one day. The court would confiscate his dough and she'd be left with a husband in gaol and no money.'

'And you're saying this ring was enough to change her mind?'

'No,' the three voices trilled again, exasperated by my naivety. 'She made him give it up,' Mum added.

'Give what up?'

'His criminal activities, of course. He put his money into property development instead. Mind you, that's a lot like crime anyway.' They all laughed grimly at this. 'These days he's a legitimate businessman. Pillar of the community. Even gives to charity, as long as there's a photographer close by to snap him handing over the cheque. But I tell you, she played hard to get until he agreed. Made him give her that ring to show he was serious.' Mum spoke as though she knew all about it. 'A sort of …' She reached for a word, not quite able to grasp it.

'A symbol,' said Mrs Duval, helping her out. 'A symbol that he'd stick to the bargain.'

'Exactly,' said my mother. 'And the way that marriage has gone ever since, I bet she has to keep looking at it on her finger to remind herself that he's worth it.' The tone of her voice changed, becoming more furtive, so that her next words sounded like a secret revealed. 'You know Marilyn Banisch, who has her hair done here? She cleans for the Sidebottoms, and from what she's told me, the lovely Narelle has threatened to leave him several times over the years. She went for him with a kitchen knife once when he was caught with his pants down. Of course, what scares old Terry most is a divorce. She'd take him to the cleaners, well and truly. It would make what he spent on the ring look like chicken feed.'

'Her father wouldn't mind,' Veronica commented. 'He hates Terry, and he wouldn't mind a cashed-up daughter back in the family business, either.'

'Family business?' I asked, becoming confused.

'The lovely Narelle was a Linacre. Her father was as big a crook as Sidebottom. That Narelle, she'd seen the court cases and the gaol sentences first hand. They're all bent, that lot,' Mum added savagely. 'There were the Fergusons, too, and the Meaghers.'

'The Meaghers!' I shot a glance at Glenda, who had finally stopped chuckling to herself. She nodded seriously. I had to be careful here. Luckily, Mum didn't think it odd that I knew the name. She just ploughed on. 'Yes, the Meaghers and the Linacres. You see them down at Ferguson's garage. They're all related, and all shady in one way or another.'

'All shady?' That was a bit rich. Just because some family members are crooked it doesn't mean they all are. Look at Mum herself. Her own father was banged up at that very moment, yet she is straight as a die. Doesn't even fiddle the taxes for Hair by Sinclair, much to Uncle Bruce's disgust.

Damn. Mention of Uncle Bruce ruined my whole argument.

But which way did Chris Meagher lean? Was he part of the 'family business' or was he honest? From the way they were talking, the Meagher family must be into crimes a lot more serious than the minor bit of wealth redistribution that Grandad got up to. But how was I going to find out? If I asked for details Mum would want to know why I was so interested. I risked one vague question. 'So how are the Meaghers related to Mrs Sidebottom?'

Immediately Glenda gave me the eye, which was hardly surprising when I was supposed to have sworn off Chris just yesterday.

The ladies considered my question. 'It was the sister, wasn't it?' Veronica said finally, checking for confirmation among the others. They threw names around for a couple of minutes, each one leading to another web of connections. I became hopelessly confused, but not before I had worked out that Chris Meagher's father must be Narelle Sidebottom's cousin, or something like that. Not what you'd call close.

God, I hope he's not a crook …

NINETEEN

WHEN I SWITCHED THE MOBILE back on later I found the 'Eisenberg twins' had left a message for me. At least they weren't afraid of the robot voice on the answering machine like Mrs Foat, but that's about all I can say for them.

'Hello, Rosie. It's Deirdre Eisenberg. We need some help tomorrow to get our bears to the bazaar.'

Bears to the bazaar?

Rain had started to fall by the time I presented myself at their door on Tuesday morning, only to find it answered by a teddy bear. 'Is that you, Rosie?' the bear asked me. It was enormous, maybe a metre high, though it was sitting in midair with its huge feet pointing straight at my belly button. The voice was coming from behind it. Caroline's face appeared over its shoulder. 'Here, take this out to the car, would you?' She pushed the huge thing into my arms so that I had to hug it to stop it from falling. Luckily it was very light, and now that I had recovered from the surprise it was a wonderful feeling having a soft and furry bear in my arms. I snuggled my face into its chest and thought of ... well, all right, I thought of Chris Meagher, who could be as cute as a teddy bear, I was sure, even if I hadn't seen much of that side of him yet.

'Come along, Rosie. Get moving. There's quite a lot to carry.' The lounge room, I noticed through the doorway, was densely populated with teddy bears of all sizes, most a honey-brown and much smaller than the one I had embraced so heartily. I gave the big one a name, Christian, and carried him out to the Mercedes, where I took a cruel delight in dunking him straight into the boot.

A huge screech followed. 'Not in the boot, dear!' Deirdre scolded from beneath an umbrella.

'*Of course* it can go in the boot,' said Caroline, who wasn't quite so sentimental.

I could see what was coming. If I let them enjoy another argument, we'd just get wherever we were going in time to come back again. They would have had a thoroughly delightful outing, but I wanted some results from my labours and I certainly wasn't going to stand around getting wet.

So I sat Christian the giant teddy bear in the front seat, with the seat belt buckled in place. Even Caroline smiled.

The boot was quickly filled with sack after sack of teddy bears, much smaller than Christian, thank heavens, leaving just two medium-sized specimens, which went onto the back seat with the Eisenberg sisters, one in each lap. (The bears on top.)

By this time I had worked out what was happening. Every third Tuesday of the month, the well-meaning ladies of Prestwidge held a charity bazaar on the footpath outside The Grove. It was full of the sorts of stuff no-one can do without: little lace doilies, wall hangings croqueted from plastic bread packets, pin boards made from wine corks. Don't know how I could miss it, really.

'Do you make these bears yourselves?' I asked as we set out.

They beamed proudly into my rear-view mirror, in agreement for once. Not that it lasted. 'I do the design and the cutting out,' said Deirdre, 'and Caroline does the finishing.'

'I design them too, Deirdre. That one you have in your lap is one of my creations, start to finish.'

'No, not quite, Caroline. You've forgotten that I …'

Spare me! I checked the side mirror, because I couldn't see anything but fake fur and frozen smiles in the other. Normally I wouldn't have taken any particular notice of the cars behind me, but filling the whole mirror was a silver-grey Commodore. Its windows were heavily tinted, giving it the air of a cool dude in his shades.

That was odd. I had thought the same thing about a car parked in our street as I drove off this morning.

Oh, shit! No wonder I'd had the same thought. It was the same car!

I changed lanes. So did the silver Commodore. Wait a minute, I thought. I've seen this car before, not only this morning but a week ago as well. This was the car that had cut in on me so recklessly just after my first outing with the Eisenbergs, almost causing an accident.

I turned right and, three blocks later, left into Pine Street. The Commodore was still there.

I didn't bother with any of the intermediate stages. I went straight to panic. What was I going to do? That horrible voice had lost patience. He had come after me to get the ring, a ring I still didn't have and had no way of getting. I had two old ladies in the car with me. What would happen to them if he forced me off the road? I could see the headlines. 'DEATH AMONG THE TEDDY BEARS'. 'ELDERLY WOMEN DIE IN ARMS OF FURRY COMPANIONS'.

Then I saw it through the misting windshield: the grimy sign pointing to Ferguson's Auto Centre. According to Mum this was the criminal hub of Prestwidge, but I was desperate. I pulled rapidly off the road, splashed carelessly through a puddle, and came to a sudden halt beside one of the pumps. A face appeared round the end of the workshop, a very ugly but slightly familiar face. It disappeared, and a few seconds later Chris Meagher stepped into the rain, wiping grease from his hands onto a rag.

I rolled down the window in time to hear him say, 'I didn't expect to see you here, Rosie. Look, about the other night …'

'Don't worry about that now. I haven't come looking for an apology.'

'Do you need petrol, then?'

'No!'

He didn't know whether to smirk or take offence at my tone, and seemed to settle for eyeing me suspiciously. 'What's wrong?'

'I just need somewhere to … shelter.'

'From the rain, eh, in case it melts the Merc's paintwork, is that it?' Obviously he had learned a few lesson in sarcasm from Mr Hoskins. Understandable, since he had probably spent more time in the Deputy Principal's office than I did, if he was anything like the rest of his family.

All this time, I couldn't help staring over my shoulder, craning my neck, trying to see out onto the road.

Chris's sarcasm disappeared as soon as he noticed. 'Is someone after you?'

'Shh,' I said, a little too loudly, and nodded my head towards the back seat. He leaned in for a closer look and I caught the smell of him as he hovered over me. Oh, boy. But this was no time for such pleasures. He spotted the Eisenberg sisters with a teddy bear each on their laps. They didn't have a clue what was going on, but they had been brought up by their ghastly mother to be polite. 'Hello,' they said together, giving a cheery if rather forced smile.

'You're being followed, eh,' blabbered Chris, letting the cat out of the bag. 'It's not a bunch of little green teddy bears from Mars, is it?' Sensitive concern was gone. Sarcasm was back. As for Caroline and Deirdre, they both took a worried glance through the window behind them but didn't notice any Martian stuffed toys.

'Rosie, how long are we going to be stopped here?' asked Deirdre. 'We don't want to be late for the bazaar.'

They had a point. I couldn't hang around here all day. But the silver Commodore could be waiting round the corner. If I went back out onto the road, I could be right back where I'd started.

'Do you want me to ride shotgun,' Chris suggested.

'What?' I didn't have a clue what he was talking about.

'Shotgun was the name for a guard on a stagecoach. Haven't you ever seen any old westerns on TV?'

Yeah, yeah, I thought to myself, without really thinking. Hey, wait! He's offering to help me! 'Get in,' I said quickly.

He knew better than to ask if he could drive. When he opened the passenger-side door he found his namesake occupying the space. 'Cute.'

I stabbed at the seat-belt buckle to free the bear. Chris slipped onto the seat and lifted Teddy Christian to balance on his knee. 'You'll get done for overloading,' he quipped.

'Shut up,' I growled under my breath like an angry bear (grizzly, not teddy).

'This'll be a fun date. Two chaperones in the back seat and a bear the size of Alaska on my knee. Give us a kiss, beautiful,' he urged the bear.

'It's a he.'

'Just my luck.'

Luck? I was thinking about *the bear's* luck. If it could have driven, I'd happily have swapped places.

'What kind of car was following you?' he asked, more serious now as he saw the way I was throwing the Merc around in the traffic.

'A silver Commodore.'

Somehow he manoeuvred himself into a position where he could see into the wing mirror. 'Yeah, I see it.'

'What!' My reckless turning hadn't left a moment to look into the rear-view mirror. I did now, and there it was.

'V8,' Chris commented with a hint of admiration. 'Why's he following you?'

'There's a good reason, but I can't explain right now.'

'Where are you going?'

'I don't know. I'm just going.'

'Well, take it easy, will you, before you have a prang. He's just trying to scare you.'

'And doing a great job.'

'No, I mean it. If he really wanted to hurt you, he'd have jumped you by now.'

Oh, great. I felt a lot better now. Chris contorted himself again to keep track of the Commodore. 'You're not going to outrun him in this. Head up onto Maplethorpe as though you're going across to Martindale.'

'I don't want to end up in Martindale!'

'Just do it.'

There was a certain authority in his voice now, so I obeyed. Maybe he had a plan, which put him one step ahead of me. Once onto Maplethorpe I had to speed up, because it's a major road with a higher speed limit. If the Commodore wanted to force us into a ditch, this would have been the perfect place.

'Stay in the left lane,' he commanded. 'Good, now the Commodore's three cars back. This is what you do. The road divides up ahead. Just before we get to that point, I want you to pull off the road, here on the left-hand side, and stop as fast as you can. There's a bit of gravel, so you might slide for a few metres, but you'll manage.'

'But the cars behind me …'

'They'll get a fright, but so what? Ready?' There was a dreadful silence for a few moments, then, 'NOW!'

I yanked the wheel and took us suddenly onto the side of the road. There was a brief screech of brakes, and one driver blared his horn, but as the Merc jerked to a halt I saw that the silver Commodore had been forced to continue on in the traffic.

'Great work, Rosie!' said Chris, clearly impressed. 'Perfect position.' He pointed across the bitumen to a concrete barrier that blocked off one side of the road from the other. We weren't quite level with where it began.

'What now?'

Chris was already looking behind us as best he could. 'As soon as this next lot of traffic's gone past, hang a U-turn and head back the way we came.'

'He'll do the same, won't he?'

'He can't. At least not for the next two kilometres. That's how far that concrete barrier goes. I'll bet he's hit the gas by now, but it won't do him any good. We're out of here.'

I pressed down on the accelerator. 'You're a genius! How did you think of that?'

'Professional secret.'

Yeah, and just exactly which profession is that? I wanted to ask.

'Er ... excuse me,' said a timid voice from the back. 'Could we please go to the bazaar now?'

I looked across at Chris, who was still holding that lucky bear lightly on his knee. 'You'll have to drop them somewhere,' he said.

That settled it. I headed towards The Grove and the aptly named bazaar. At least it had stopped raining now, so the Eisenberg sisters wouldn't have to stand about under umbrellas. Passing cars sprayed mist from their tyres onto the Merc's windshield, but when I flicked on the wipers a smear of mud made it even harder to see. 'There's a button or something for water, isn't there?' I asked Chris.

He showed me, and instantly a stream of water shot straight at my nose, only to dissipate over the windscreen and splash playfully off the wipers. 'Ah, that's better.'

So it was, but what was that noise? I'd never heard anything like it before. I sent a worried glance towards Chris.

'It's not the engine,' he said.

The noise stopped, but as soon as I turned on that jet of water again it was back.

'When was the last time you put water in the reservoir?' Chris asked, with the tone of a dentist asking how often you brushed your teeth.

'I didn't even know it had a reservoir for this kind of thing.'

'Typical,' he said contemptuously, but I knew he was stifling a good-natured laugh. 'You've got something in there. Look, it's interfering with the flow.'

As he spoke, the stream of water spluttered, then returned to normal, then spluttered again. 'Pull over,' he said.

I completed this manoeuvre with a little more respect for the road rules than on my last attempt. Chris was quickly out of the car, pulling up the hood and securing it in place. I got out to watch, just as he reached into the engine compartment and released a square plastic container from its clips. With his hand over the opening, he turned it upside down and let the last of the water drain through his fingers. But when he lifted the container, something remained on his palm, something that glistened in the weak sunlight doing its best to break through the clouds. *It was the missing ring!*

'I can't believe it! The ring! Thank God! My grandad will be OK now.'

'What are you talking about?' Chris asked. 'And what the hell was a ring doing in the windscreen washer's reservoir?'

'It's a long story,' I replied, plucking the ring from his palm, 'but I've been looking for this for ages. I've searched the car with a fine-toothed comb. Even looked here, under the bonnet, but I didn't see where he could have hidden it.'

'Who? Who'd want to hide a ring in your grandfather's car?'

'Not just *any* ring. Look, we'll get the Eisenberg sisters to their bazaar and then I'll explain.'

Before I could move, Caroline poked her head out of the back window. 'Your phone's ringing, Rosie dear.'

The dreaded mobile! I snatched it from the dashboard, where it had been lurking silently all this time. I didn't care if it *was* that sinister voice now. In fact, I hoped it was, and then I could get rid of the damn ring once and for all. 'Hello?'

'Thought you'd lost me, did you?' said a voice. It wasn't the one I was expecting, but the tone was much the same. The words alone told me it was the guy who'd been following me. But I had the ring now, and I was feeling confident. 'Er, excuse me,' I said rather brazenly. 'We *did* lose you.'

'Think again, sister,' his voice sneered.

I didn't like the sound of that.

'Rosie,' Chris called anxiously from behind me. I turned and found him nodding up the street. I followed his gaze and there was the Commodore. The bastard even flashed his lights at me. Cute.

'You've found the ring, haven't you?'

What should I say? This wasn't the man who had been threatening me. It could be anyone, someone not connected to those other calls at all. The whole world seemed to know that the missing ring was somewhere in the black Mercedes, and this guy had probably seen us find it. But if I gave him the ring I might be signing Grandad's death warrant.

'Listen,' said the voice. 'This is very easy. There's no-one around. No-one to watch. You just put the ring down on the kerb where you're standing and drive off. Then I come down and collect it. Done. You don't even have to lay eyes on me.'

Think! Think! Just when you need it most, your mind goes blank on you. I never was good under pressure. 'OK,' I said lamely. 'You win. I'm putting the ring on the kerb now.' I walked round beside the car and bent down. 'There,' I said. 'Come and get it.'

Chris looked at me rather strangely, but he slipped back into the seat with his furry namesake as soon as I headed for the driver's door. The engine started up and I took off, lurching the poor Eisenberg sisters and their teddy bears backwards in their seats.

'What did he tell you to do?' asked Chris.

'To leave the ring on the kerb for him to collect.'

'That's why you bent down?'

I nodded.

'But you didn't leave it there. I saw you put it in your pocket.'

'Yeah, I know — and is he ever going to be pissed off when he finds out.'

TWENTY

THE MOST IMPORTANT THING NOW was to dump the Eisenberg sisters before the Commodore caught up with us. As a matter of fact, I didn't want to think about what would happen when it did. But first the sisters. The Grove wasn't far ahead. In fact, travelling at the speed I'd managed to get out of the old Merc, we were closing in fast. There were the tables set out along the side of the road leading into the shopping precinct. 'I'll drop you two off here,' I called into the back seat. 'It'll be a bit of a rush, I'm afraid.'

I pulled up in a No Standing zone, hoping that Chris and I could jettison the sisters and their bears without attracting the attention of the parking Nazis.

But luck deserted me. I was barely out of door when who should turn up but Constable Enright himself. 'You can't park there,' he informed me with barely concealed delight.

'I'm not parking. I'm just stopping long enough to unload some gear for the bazaar.'

'Makes no difference. You're blocking traffic. You have to move on *right now*.'

'But it will only take a second. If you'd help us instead of standing there quoting the law ...' This was perhaps going a bit far, considering I wasn't exactly Constable Enright's favourite human being after our last encounter.

'MOVE THE CAR!' he hollered. To make matters worse, he came and stood beside the boot so that we couldn't open it. A bit of poetic justice on his part, I suppose.

There was nothing else for it. I considered bursting into helpless feminine tears, but it would have been such a pathetic cop-out, even as a last resort.

Then things got worse. The silver Commodore suddenly swung round the corner and screeched to halt behind the Merc. Of course, this created a bit of commotion, which Constable Enright didn't appreciate. He marched over to the Commodore, intent on having a very large piece of this miscreant. When he did this, he left Chris and me to our own devices. I opened the boot and Chris grabbed the sacks of teddy bears. The sisters themselves were already out of the car, bears in hand, and fuzzy

Christian had been extracted from the front seat so that he now sat casually on his arse on the pavement, watching us all fuss about.

The door of the Commodore opened and out stepped a young man in a badly cut suit. He headed straight for me, like a dog going for the juiciest bone.

'Hey, you!' Enright called to him. 'Get back here! You can't leave this car here like this.'

The guy ignored him and kept coming towards me. I wasn't going to stand there like a zombie and let him grab me, so I took off, and that's why my recollections of what followed contain a few gaps, but this is what I saw, along with the rest which I've guessed.

Constable Enright kept up his wailing like a kid no-one will play with in the schoolyard. Fat lot of use he was. It was Chris who saved the day. While I scuttled away into the crowd, he stepped straight into the guy's path. By the time I turned around again, there was a figure sitting on his bum looking dazed. It wasn't Christian the teddy bear, and it certainly wasn't the real Christian, who stood over the unfortunate figure in the stance you see in bad Kung Fu movies.

I had my own priorities to attend to, so I turned away. I had to do something about the ring. Hide it, dump it, get rid of it somehow. But where?

I was right next to the row of little tables and stalls, but I could hardly drop the ring unnoticed among the plastic flowers or the picture frames decorated with seashells. Just as I began to despair, I saw precisely what I needed. One of the stalls sold tacky costume jewellery: brooches, bracelets and rack after rack of cheap rings set with hunks of coloured glass instead of rubies and emeralds. I waited for the right moment and slipped the ring onto one of the velvet trays. Phew! *That* was done. The thug from the silver Commodore could catch me now and there would be no ring for him to find.

Using the canvas on the stalls to stay out of sight, I crept back as close as I dared. Enright had finally realised that if he wanted to play with the other children he had to move away from the cars, so he could get into the thick of it. 'I know you!' he was shouting at my pursuer. 'Kenny something, isn't it? I've seen you down at the station. What do you think you're doing?'

Kenny Something was on his feet again, but he'd forgotten all about me by then and he didn't bother to acknowledge the policeman either. His hard, narrow eyes were fixed firmly on Chris. 'I'm going to do you, Meagher,' he growled.

Oh, great. So they *all* knew each other. One big, happy family, and because this was Prestwidge, capital of the dysfunctional family, they all seemed bent on physical violence towards one another.

Kenny lunged at Chris, who evaded him easily, but it was the last straw for Constable Enright. I don't know exactly which crime Kenny was arrested for, Attempted Assault (if there is such an offence) or Illegal Parking or Being a Pain in the Arse. In the end I think Enright nabbed him for Disrespect to a Police Officer.

This was a real break for me, but nothing ever works out the way you want it to. Even with Kenny struggling in a pair of handcuffs, Enright spotted me in my hiding place and started shouting at me. 'This is a No Stopping zone! You're holding up the traffic flow!' We all looked around. There was barely a car in sight, but that only seemed to make Constable Enright madder than he already was. Kenny squirmed even harder, and received an elbow to the guts for his trouble.

'I'm *ordering* you. Move that Mercedes now, or you'll come along with Kenny here.'

All right, all right. I thought it prudent to move the Mercedes to the car park before the poor man blew a foo-foo valve. I beckoned to Chris and jumped in myself on the driver's side.

'Jeez, Rosie, you're driving this thing like a Formula One racer,' Chris complained as I threw the Merc around the car park.

'I left the ring on one of the stalls.'

'You what!'

'I had to get rid of it in case he caught me. It'll still be there when we get back.' But if I was so confident about that, why was I hurtling round like a maniac?

I shoved the Merc haphazardly into a disabled parking space (sorry, it was an emergency) and set off back to the stalls, walking quickly at first, then jogging and finally sprinting along the concrete ramps. OK, there were the stalls, and I wasted no time in heading over to get the ring back.

It was gone.

'*What do you mean you sold it?*' I shouted at the poor woman who ran the junk jewellery stall.

'Well, that's what a bazaar is for, isn't it?'

I hate logical people. 'But it wasn't yours to sell.'

'I thought it looked a bit strange. I don't normally make things like that.'

While I went berserk, Chris kept his head. 'Who did you sell it to?' he asked calmly.

I could have kissed him. In fact, maybe later I would anyway, whether we found the ring or not.

'An elderly lady. Seen her before, I'm sure of it.'

Oh, that was useful. We waited while the lady racked her brains trying to remember. 'No,' she said finally. 'It's gone.'

I was ready to strangle her until *she* was gone — permanently.

Chris continued to be the steady one. 'Can you see her around the place still?'

The lady took off her glasses, folded them carefully into their case and put on another pair. Meanwhile, my heart had sunk around my knees. But I shouldn't have doubted her. Didn't I take a bunch of old people around in Grandad's car? Didn't they amaze me from time to time? 'There she is!' said the lady. She pointed behind us. 'The one in the blue floral dress. I remember *I* had a nice dress like that once.'

I didn't wait to hear about it. I was off after the blue floral dress. The woman had just gone through the doors and reached the first of the shops, walking slowly, glancing into the gleaming windows as she passed. Thirty metres, twenty. When I was just ten metres away I stopped, and Chris almost bowled me over from behind. 'What's the matter?'

'I know who it is,' I said, smiling. This wasn't going to be so hard after all. I relaxed and caught my breath, and let my heart come back up from my ankles and into my chest, where it could slow down a little. 'Her name's Janice Duval.'

'Janice! Janice!' I called brightly.

Mrs Duval heard me and turned around. 'Oh, hello, Rosie.' There was that charming smile that had fooled me so completely.

'How did you get here? If I'd known you needed to go shopping I could have given you a lift.'

'Oh, Eric and I impose upon you far too much,' she said sincerely. 'I try to be independent from time to time. I got a lift with Mrs Benson, who runs the second-hand stall. Eric stayed at home. He's been rather tired these last few days.'

I'll bet!

It was time to get down to business. 'Janice, you just bought a ring from the costume jewellery stall, didn't you?'

'As a matter of fact, I did. It's a lovely piece. Much better than you usually find on a stall like that.' She took it out of her handbag and slipped it onto her finger, where it glittered in the gaudy fluorescent light of The Grove. 'How did *you* know?'

'Well, that's just it. It's mine, actually.'

'What do you mean? How could it be yours, dear? It was for sale on the stall. Are you saying it was stolen from you?'

'Er ... no,' I said pathetically. Damn. I hadn't thought this through (just like the rest of my life). 'I mean, it was *meant* to be mine.'

'You were going to buy it, is that what you're saying?'

That was as good an opening as any. Then if she felt she owed me anything for driving her around, she would be obliged to let me have it. I smiled. 'Yes, I was going to buy it.'

'Then you were too late, dear. I'm awfully sorry, but I beat you to it and I don't feel inclined to part with it.' She stretched out her hand, palm downwards, admiring the ring. Look at it, for God's sake! The diamond was the size of an egg. No wonder it was worth twenty thousand dollars.

Chris leaned down to whisper in my ear. 'Let me talk to her.'

I was startled, as much by the intimacy of his movement as the offer he had made. I stepped back automatically and saw him close in on Mrs Duval like a predator on its quarry, those honey-golden curls just touching the shoulders of his T-shirt.

Though I was officially excluded from this conversation, fortunately I could hear most of it from where I was standing.

'Mrs Duval, it wasn't Rosie who was going to buy

the ring. It was me. She just loves it, you see, and I wanted to buy if for her, to show her how much I like her. I would have bought it as soon as I saw it, but I didn't have a dollar in my pocket. We had to go off to the automatic teller to get the cash, and by the time we came back …'

'I had bought it instead,' she finished for him.

I was amazed. Such charm! He'd lied so smoothly that even I almost believed him. She would *have* to give him the ring now.

We both waited patiently for her to cough it up.

Nope. She wouldn't budge.

He tried again. 'It might look nice, but you're a mature woman, Mrs Duval, and it's not like it's real or anything. People will know that it's just a cheap piece of costume jewellery and well, they can be cruel sometimes. They'll laugh at you behind your back. But Rosie, she's young. It's the kind of thing young girls wear, the kind of thing their boyfriends give them. She'd be so proud of it, and it would make both of us very happy if she could have it.'

I was convinced. How could *anyone* hold out after that?

Mrs Duval considered Chris's fine words as she gazed down at the ring. 'No, you're wrong, young man. I'm not embarrassed at all by this ring, and of course I know it's a cheap imitation. Look,' she said suddenly, and before we could stop her, she turned to scrape the diamond down the glass of the shop window.

Oh, God, that's torn it, I thought. She'll see the scratch it leaves and know she's got far more of a bargain than she ever imagined. Chris and I held our breath.

Phew! She was an old woman and she hadn't pressed hard enough on the glass to leave a mark.

'There, you see? But I don't care what people think. I like it.'

'What did you pay for it?' Chris asked, his charm offensive now almost spent.

'Fifteen dollars.'

'I'll give you thirty for it.'

'No, and don't waste your breath offering me any more. The ring is not for sale.' And she walked off at a steady pace into The Grove.

Chris turned back to me. 'Sorry,' he said, defeated. 'What do we do now? It's a bit late to mug her.' (I'm pretty sure that was a joke.)

Maybe my mind isn't so useless after all, because I already knew *exactly* what we were going to do. Mrs Duval had turned us down flat, even when Chris pulled at her heartstrings with that cock-and-bull story of romance. It was time to get tough. 'Wait here,' I said.

'You won't change her mind now,' he called.

'You wanna bet?' I shot back at him, my jaw already setting hard.

I was back in three minutes flat with the precious ring in my pocket. Chris had been watching from twenty metres away and saw Mrs Duval pull the ring from her finger and drop it meekly into my palm.

192

'That's incredible. She just handed it over, no arguments,' he said, open-mouthed. 'You didn't even give her the fifteen dollars back. What in God's name did you say to her?'

'I can't tell you. I have to be discreet.'

'What does *that* mean?'

'Let's just say I know some things about Mrs Duval that she'd like me to keep a secret.'

Sometimes I can be *so* smug.

TWENTY-ONE

CHRIS WAS SILENT AT FIRST on the way back to the garage. 'Could I have a look at that ring?' he asked finally.

'No. It's in my pocket and that's where it's staying for now.' He went silent again and I felt awful for speaking so bluntly. 'Look, thanks so much for helping me. If it hadn't been for you, that Kenny guy might have taken it from me.' Pause. 'You know him, don't you?'

'He's muscle for hire, all brawn and no brains. Used to hang around Prestwidge big-noting himself when I was still at school. But he ended up in trouble with the cops so often, it got too hot for him here. He moved on to greener pastures, where no-one knew him.'

'Only now, he's back,' I pointed out.

'And he's after that ring in your pocket,' Chris added. 'Listen, Rosie. It's not yours, is it? In fact, I'm pretty sure I know who it belongs to.'

'A relative of yours,' I told him, to show that I was still ahead of the game.

'Well, well,' he said, staring at me. He looked genuinely impressed.

'Are you going to dob me in to the Sidebottoms?'

'Not me. Narelle's not exactly my favourite relative. But if that ring is causing you grief, maybe it would be better if she *did* get it back. Anonymously. I could arrange that for you, no worries.'

It was tempting, but it would hardly solve the problem of Grandad's safety. I explained to Chris about the sinister phone calls.

'I don't like the sound of it, Rosie. Some of those guys play rough.'

'I know. I'm just trying to make sure my grandad isn't the one they play with.'

He scowled. 'I'll ask around about Kenny. Maybe someone will tell me who he's working for.'

'Thanks, but don't worry too much,' I assured him. 'It's nearly over now. I have the ring. The next time Mr Underworld calls, I can arrange to let him have it. Then Grandad will be safe.'

'Mr Underworld? You can make jokes about it all you like, Rosie, but those sorts of people aren't like you see on television, I can tell you that.'

I didn't like the way he sounded so familiar with the subject. But now we'd arrived back at Fergo's garage.

'Do you want to top up the tank? Could be down a millimetre or two.'

'Very funny.'

'Take the Merc round the side of the workshop,' he told me, as though this were a real taxi and I were just another driver. Who could refuse such a gracious invitation, especially when there was nowhere else to park? We pulled up next to a gleaming red sports coupé — mag wheels, spoiler ... the complete testosterone dream.

'This is what we were supposed to go out in the other night.'

'You're joking. You mean it's *yours*?'

He didn't answer, with words or even a smile. He didn't have to.

To be honest, I was very impressed. This wasn't a Prestie Grunt-mobile like the one those yobbos were driving on the way to our date at The Grove. I could feel myself falling for the image, the style, the cool.

Just in time, a little voice called from inside my head. *Hey, sister, don't get carried away, because there'll be a catch here somewhere.* And it didn't take me long to think of one. The Linacres, the Fergusons, the Meaghers ... if the gossip around Hair by Sinclair was even half right, these families made Paddy Larkin look like a model citizen. I'm not squeamish and I'm certainly no saint, but I didn't want to get mixed up with a guy who made a living out of other people's misery.

'What do you do for a living, Chris?'

'A lot of things. You might say I'm an odd-job man.'

'Since when can an odd-job man afford a sports car?'

He hit me with that trademark smirk. 'Depends on how odd the jobs are.'

I looked to the left and then to right, like I was about to cross the street. There was no-one to hear us, but all the same, I came closer so that I wouldn't have to raise my voice. That doesn't mean my voice lacked a certain edge, if you know what I mean. 'Tell me straight. Do you deal drugs? 'Cause if you're a dealer, I don't want anything to do with you.'

He looked like I'd pulled a knife on him. The smirk was gone, replaced by an expression he hadn't let me see before. I realised it was the real Chris Meagher, when he let the cool, the toughness and the teasing slip. He was thinking how to answer me, and I could tell from that look it was important to him that I believed him. 'Rosie, I don't do drugs and I don't deal them either.'

'So what *do* you do?'

'I told you. Odd jobs, but not handyman stuff or mowing lawns or anything.' I must have looked sceptical. 'And I don't rob banks, either. Look, I'm not trying to pretend that everything I do is a hundred per cent legal, but *you're* hardly the one to talk.'

No, that was true. I was Paddy Larkin's granddaughter, and at that particular moment I was carrying a twenty-thousand-dollar ring in my pocket that had been stolen from Farr's Fine Jewellery.

I hate it when boys are right. It robs a girl of her rightful authority. Besides, he had convinced me on the drug bit and he knew it, too.

'So, do you want to come for a ride some time?'

I guessed what was coming. He might have just helped me out with Kenny in the silver Commodore, but that was the least he could have done after last Saturday night. 'We'll just pretend last Saturday night didn't happen.'

'I've got a hole in my brand-new skirt that says it did.'

'I'm sorry, Rosie,' he said, offering an apology at last. I had been starting to wonder if the word was part of his vocabulary. 'Come on, say yes. Saturday night will be wiped from existence. We can make a new start.'

Come on, strength, girl, strength. I thought of my ruined skirt. I thought of Christian, the giant teddy bear balancing on a certain knee, then made myself stop. I thought of Glenda, who would probably never speak to me again if she found out.

I looked at Chris in his jeans and muscle-hugging T-shirt. No contest. What did Glenda know, anyway? 'Yeah, all right,' I said.

Bloody hormones.

It was time I spoke to Glenda again though, not because I had a guilty conscience. In fact, I had already decided to extend my new-found taste for discretion to my own love life as well. But Glenda needed to know I'd found the ring.

She was lounging about reading trashy magazines when I arrived, but she somehow managed to drag herself away from the lives of Hollywood stars, especially when I told her I'd been involved in a car chase. To be honest, I lied just a little. I told her the whole story as accurately as I could, but left a certain Christian Meagher out completely. Therefore, it was *my* idea to lose the silver Commodore on Maplethorpe Road (I saw it on TV, I explained) and *my* educated ear that picked up a problem with the windscreen washer. Glenda looked a bit sceptical when I got to that part, but I showed her the ring and that settled it.

'Holy shit! I've never seen a diamond that size before.' She took it from me for a closer look, and before she even realised what she was doing it was on her finger. It's a girl thing, maybe. I'd already tried it on myself and decided that it was a bit ostentatious. (Look it up!) 'There's one thing that doesn't sound right, though,' she said, moving towards the window. 'You said it didn't leave a scratch when Mrs Whatsername tried it on the glass?'

'No, thank God. Otherwise we would never have got it back.'

'But Rosie, you don't have to press very hard to scratch glass with a diamond.' She was standing close to the window by now, and after she had checked that no-one was looking in from the street, she did her best to gouge a tiny groove in the bottom corner. 'Nothing,' she said.

'That can't be right.' I came over to watch as she tried it a second time. She wasn't as careful with the window on this attempt, and drew the ring right along the bottom, near the frame. No mark.

'There's something wrong here. One of the dancers I work with did the same thing with her engagement ring. Made a complete mess of the mirror in the ladies'. The diamond was tiny compared with this one, but it did the job. If I didn't know any better I'd say this is a fake.'

'Can't be,' I insisted. 'Here, give it to me.' But pressing as hard as I could, the sharpest point of the diamond barely made an impression.

'It's not real,' Glenda announced with certainty, after I'd struggled for a couple of minutes.

'I don't believe you,' I said firmly. All this fuss, the threats to Grandad, Kenny trailing me in the silver Commodore. The ring *had* to be real. 'This isn't exactly a scientific test,' I pointed out. Still, I had to admit my confidence was shaken.

Then the phone rang. I stabbed at the Answer button and just listened. There was no need to try my desert-dry vocal chords, because Mr Underworld launched straight into another tirade.

'What the hell do you think you're doing? You've got the ring, and there's no point denying it any more. My man saw you find it in the engine compartment this morning. So what are you playing at, pretending to leave it for him and then taking off like that?'

'How was I supposed to know he was working for *you*? Could have been anyone! I took off to make sure the ring didn't fall into the wrong hands.' What was I doing? This made it sound like I was on his side — working for him, in fact.

'You're not doing your dear old grandad any favours here, you know. Believe me, he's the one who'll pay.'

But this cruel threat didn't frighten me so much as make me angry, and when I'm angry I tend to say a few things that are best left unsaid. (Hey, it's a personality thing.) 'Look, I can't wait to let you have the bloody ring! I don't want it. It's a fake, anyway!'

Now, I wasn't exactly convinced of that myself at this point, and I certainly didn't expect him to believe it. It would just sound like a pathetic attempt to put him off. But what the heck, I was steaming ahead like a runaway train, and just as hard to stop. 'It doesn't cut glass, you know. We've tried it.'

Come on, I thought. Laugh at me. Tell me I'm a fool, that I don't know what I'm talking about.

Nothing. Complete silence from Mr Underworld.

Glenda had been spending the last thirty seconds making desperate signals with her hands and face, trying to shut me up. But she couldn't shut my brain down. It was working overtime, and suddenly out popped the answer, like I was one of those clunky computers the size of a fridge that spit out cards with the right solution to a maths problem in old TV shows. 'You already knew it was a fake, didn't you?' I said into the mobile.

'Shit!' said Mr Underworld, and the phone went dead.

I stared down at the silent thing in my hand. 'He hung up,' I told Glenda, but before we could even move, the phone trilled again.

'Now you listen here, girl. I don't know where you got that stupid idea. The ring you've got there is real and it's worth a lot of money. Most of all, it's worth your grandfather's safety. *That's* what you have to worry about. Now, the young idiot I sent to follow you is being bailed out at this very minute, and once he gets his car out of the police compound, he's going to …'

He didn't finish, at least not in my hearing he didn't. I'd cut the call. Before he could ring back, I turned off the mobile altogether.

'Do you really think I'm right?' Glenda asked. She still had the ring in her hand, turning it over and over as though this would settle the matter. 'Is this a fake after all?'

'Try it on the glass again,' I suggested. Despite my performance on the phone, I really *wanted* the damn thing to be real. Life would be much less complicated if it was.

'NO,' said Glenda with a Paddy Larkin firmness. 'There's only one way to find out if it's real or fake. We'll have to take it to a jeweller.'

Problem. How to get a valuation done on a stolen ring that might be worth twenty thousand dollars when there's no way I look old enough to own such a thing.

Solution. Glenda — or at least Glenda when she is being Giselle.

'But I'm only two years older than you.'

'Yeah. And you can get away with being thirty if you want to.'

'Oh, thanks. I look ancient now, do I?'

I have to admit that saying she looked thirty was a terrible insult, but I hadn't meant it that way. 'It's the clothes, the poise, the maturity. You've got it. I haven't.'

After a few more compliments she agreed to help. In fact, dressing up for the part turned out to be fun. Glenda has a pair of red vinyl pants cut low enough on the hips to make Britney Spears blush. They are so tight she has to lie down to put them on, but when she stands up again, look out. There are only fifteen women on the planet who could get away with wearing those, and the other fourteen are supermodels. We draped a heavy belt of large gold rings around her hips, squeezed her into a strappy little top that ended at her navel and raided the shoe cupboard for her deadliest pair of stilettos.

'No, I still don't like it,' she said. She pulled open her drawer of 'professional' outfits and took out a jet-black wig. It was an obvious sort of wig, a wig that says out loud, *Hey, I'm wearing a wig*. She plonked it onto her head and let it fall easily into a kind of page-boy shape. With sunglasses in place and a slash of bright red lipstick, she looked just like Uma Thurman in *Pulp Fiction*.

It was no good going to a jewellery store around Prestwidge, or even Martindale, so I headed the black Mercedes into the city and then out a little way until the streets were lined with leafy trees and BMWs. I expected to see the ghost of old Mrs Eisenberg float by at any moment. We found a jewellery store — which wasn't hard around this suburb — and sat in the Merc for a while pretending to watch the road gang on the corner as they laid new kerbing and guttering.

'This is called casing the joint.'

'We've come to get a valuation, not to rob the place,' said Glenda.

'I know, but I heard Grandad say it once.'

'He was having you on. They only say things like that in movies.'

She was probably right, but it helped me deal with my nerves. A woman sauntered by carrying a little ball of fur. We couldn't tell whether it was a dog or a cat (or an avant-garde handbag, for that matter). 'Typical,' said Glenda with a snort. 'Even the pets round here get a free ride.' She opened the door and headed across the road, swinging her hips admirably and causing a meltdown among the burly members of the road gang.

She was gone for fifteen minutes — the longest fifteen minutes of my life. I felt like a pimple on the end of a huge nose, and for the first time I resented this beautiful old Mercedes. Why did I have to drive around in a Mafia staff car? Why couldn't it be a little Toyota or something? So many of those on the road no-one would notice me. How long would it take Kenny to get bailed out of the slammer, anyway? I expected to see that Commodore at any minute.

Thinking about the Commodore made me angry, and like I've said, when I'm angry I get a bit feisty. I needed this car to get around, so why *shouldn't* I use it? If I left it at home, Uncle Bruce would take it before I could blink, and then how would I get all those old people around to the shops and the hospital and everywhere else?

This defiance settled my nerves a little. The silver Commodore had just wanted to scare me, like Chris suggested. I doubted whether Kenny and his boss Mr Underworld, whoever he was, really wanted to hurt me. They could have done that by now. And they hadn't, because if they did I'd call the police, and it was pretty clear they didn't want that, either. No, it was obvious they wanted to sort this out with the least possible amount of fuss, and that gave me the upper hand if I could only work out how to use it.

I heard a round of whistles and rude cat calls. Glenda must be coming back. There she was, ignoring the guys as only a drop-dead gorgeous woman can do. An old duchess looked up from her table at the trendy café on the corner. If she frowned any harder in disapproval she'd burst all the seams from her last face-lift — or maybe she was just jealous. After my recent experiences with the older generation, I had to consider this as a definite possibility.

'Well?' I said, getting straight to the point as soon as she slipped back into the Mercedes beside me.

'The jeweller wants you to move your car. Right make, but too old. It's bad for his business.'

'Very funny. Is it real or fake?'

'Bit of both, actually,' she replied holding the ring up between her thumb and forefinger while she prolonged my agony. 'The setting is nine-carat gold but the diamond's not a diamond at all. If it were genuine, he thought it would be worth between eighteen and twenty thousand, depending on the quality of the stone.'

With her free hand she passed me an envelope that had the jeweller's name embossed in the corner. 'That's the valuation certificate. This ring is worth four hundred dollars.'

TWENTY-TWO

I STARTED THE ENGINE AND moved off into the mottled shade of the street ahead. A few turns and we were heading back in the general direction of Prestwidge — though I was in no hurry to get there, I must admit.

'OK. Let's review the facts,' said Glenda, taking charge, since I had to concentrate on the traffic. 'Separate out what we know for certain from the assumptions.'

She was good at this. All that university training, I suppose.

I started with, 'We know for certain now that the ring is a fake.'

'And?' Glenda was a regular Sherlock Holmes. I could tell she was going to work all the information out of me and sit back like a professor, dropping her devastating wisdom into the show when it suited her. What did I care, as long as we worked it out?

'We know it was stolen from Farr's jewellery store by a guy named McWhirter, and that when he thought he was going to be caught he hid the ring in a car he recognised. One he knew he could find later.'

'Mmm,' said Glenda thoughtfully. 'There's a bit of guesswork involved there. We don't know for sure that McWhirter ...'

'Oh, shut up,' I snapped. 'It's a fair assumption.'

'OK. I'll let it pass.'

'But why would he try so hard to hide this ring when he dumped all the rest of the jewellery in a vacant lot?' I asked.

'That goes in the *Don't Know* column for now, but come to think of it, this ring would probably be worth more than all those other little stones put together.'

'If it was real,' I pointed out.

'If it was real,' she conceded. 'So we can safely assume that McWhirter did think it was real.'

The skyscrapers of the city suddenly loomed ahead and I had to navigate through the on-ramps and feeder roads to the bypass leading to Prestwidge. The car fell silent until we were on to a clear stretch of road again and I could let the Merc find its own way home.

'And we think that the horrible guy on the phone knows the ring is a fake.'

I nodded. 'So why would he go to such lengths to get hold of it?'

'Another *Don't Know* at this stage. What else *do* we know?'

'That the ring belongs to Narelle Sidebottom.'

'No, wait a minute,' said Glenda, becoming excited. 'We know for certain that Narelle has a ring *just like* this one. We don't know that this one in my hand is actually hers.'

I was about to complain that she was splitting hairs unnecessarily when I saw the sense of what she was suggesting. 'You mean this is a copy?'

The ridiculous black wig nodded.

'But why would anyone make a copy?'

'More to the point, who?' said Glenda sagely.

There was only one obvious answer. 'The jeweller.'

Of course! Only a skilled jeweller could create a duplicate, and there was only one jeweller who'd had the opportunity. 'Mr Farr! Mrs Sidebottom took the ring in for him to fix it. It must be him!'

'Wait a moment,' Glenda warned. 'A lot of this is still guesswork.'

I knew she was right, but I didn't want to admit it. I searched for more evidence, the hard facts that Glenda was so keen on. 'The valuation,' I said suddenly, my lips moving before I even knew what I was saying. 'He valued the ring at twenty thousand dollars, but we know this one's only worth four hundred.'

'No jeweller could make a mistake like that,' said Glenda, following me with just as much enthusiasm now. 'He lied, deliberately. I'll bet he *did* make a copy, and that's the ring that was stolen. He was going to flog the original ring on the black market and give the Sidebottoms back the fake. And now he's desperate to get it back before anyone finds out.'

'That's why he sounded so worried when I said I'd take it to the police. He wants it back so he can get rid of it. If the police find out what he's done, he'll be in a cell next door to Grandad.'

It was all coming together at last. 'Mr Farr.' I breathed the name slowly, holding onto its final syllable. 'He's the guy who's been threatening me all this time. It has to be him.'

We had it worked out, though what we could do about it now that we had a prime suspect, neither of us knew. We were halfway back to Prestwidge by this time.

I'd turned the phone back on so Mrs Foat and the rest could reach me. When it rang I don't know who jumped higher, me or Glenda. She was mixed up in it now. If this was becoming a B-grade Hollywood affair, she looked more a part of it than me in that wig and the dark glasses. The phone lay on the console in the middle of the seat. While I looked for a place to pull over, she hit the Answer button and just listened.

It wasn't Mr Underworld — or should I say Mr Farr, since we now basically knew who he was. In a way, I wished it had been. I would have enjoyed telling him off.

'It's Meagher,' said Glenda, with her hand over the

phone. Sunglasses or no sunglasses, I knew what look I was getting from my passenger.

By now I had stopped the car. 'Hello, Chris,' I said, taking the phone. I had tried for a flat, disinterested tone and failed completely. In fact, I sounded positively overjoyed to hear from him, which I was, and Glenda knew it. Bloody psychologists!

'Rosie, you took a long time to answer. Are you OK? That clown Kenny hasn't turned up again, has he?'

'No, I'm safe. I've got a friend with me.' He didn't know who that friend was, and I wasn't about to tell him.

'I hope you don't mind me ringing like this,' he continued. 'I knew you had your grandad's mobile and Fergo had the number.'

'It's fine. It's kind of my phone now.'

He hesitated for a moment, as though he had suddenly forgotten why he'd rung. 'Look, I just wanted to know you were all right.' *He'd been thinking about me!* 'I was worried,' he added. *He was worried about me!* Somehow, all these hassles seemed to have a purpose now. 'If that Commodore turns up again, you head straight over here.'

'I'll remember that. Hey, Chris, you remember how Mrs Duval tried to scratch the glass with that diamond? Well, the reason it didn't leave a mark is because it's a fake.'

'You're kidding! Good-looking fake.'

I told him how we had visited another jeweller, but not much else. Discretion, eh!

'About our date,' he said suddenly. 'There's a band plays at Prestwidge Hotel on Wednesday nights. I ... er ... acquired a couple of tickets. Do you want to come along?'

'Yeah, great,' I answered quickly. 'Tomorrow night, then.'

Oops. That was a mistake. Glenda snatched off her wig and tore the sunglasses from her face. 'YOU'RE GOING OUT WITH HIM AGAIN?' she thundered, in a voice that could be heard by drivers in the traffic around us. Luckily, I'd killed the phone.

'I had to. I sort of owed it to him.'

'*Owed it to him!* Why?' she snorted.

'Because of this morning.'

'This morning? What are you talking about?'

'Well, actually, when I saw that car following me, I pulled into Fergo's garage and asked him to help me. I *might* have forgotten to mention that.'

She sniffed, and put the sunglasses back in place. 'Rosie Sinclair, your hormones don't need a leash. They need a cage.'

Now, I'm a patient person (no, honestly), but I was getting fed up with Glenda going on about Chris and my ... er ... attraction to him. It's not like I was some raving sex maniac. In fact, the 'V' word still applied to Rosie Sinclair, and I had no intention of changing my status with Chris Meagher or anyone else. Glenda and I had talked about this on many occasions and I reminded her of it again right there in the car. 'What have you got against him, anyway?

So you two had a bit of a thing back in Year Twelve or whatever. You're overplaying the spurned girlfriend role.'

'And you're in over your head,' she said bluntly. Glenda didn't often hit me with the older-and-wiser act, as though she were my big sister.

'What happened, anyway? You've never told me about it.'

'You don't want to know.'

Oh, yes I did. I was going out with him tomorrow night, and this time I was determined it wouldn't be the disaster of our last date. I pressed her a little, expecting her to maintain that rock-hard barrier she could put up where personal things were concerned. To my surprise, the wall came tumbling down.

'You want to know, do you? OK, then.' And then she told me about Chris and her, back in Year Twelve. I was lucky it was a straight road without much traffic to bump into. The car changed lanes twice without my realising. Trouble was, although she was telling me these things to put me off (and exaggerating outrageously, I'm certain), all it did at my end was send a kind of thrill through my body. Still, I had a lot to think about before tomorrow night.

The rest of the journey home was spent in a frosty silence.

TWENTY-THREE

THERE HAD BEEN A BIT of a run on teddy bears at the bazaar, and the Eisenberg sisters needed fake fur and stuffing and whatever to make some more. On Wednesday morning I took them over to Martindale, where there was a place that sold that sort of stuff. On the way they seemed remarkably chirpy and managed the entire journey without a disagreement. I was unsettled by that, and when I caught them glancing at me slyly and smirking to themselves in the back seat I knew there was something going on.

'You two have a secret of some kind. Come on, out with it.'

They gave a little shriek and turned their mouths

into a pair of prunes. The only thing they did say made it worse. 'You'll find out soon enough,' said Deirdre and received a vicious elbow in the ribs from Caroline for her troubles. 'Quiet, dear. You'll give it away.'

Oh, great. That was all I needed in my life. Another mystery.

This reminded me about the ring, which I could feel in my pocket at that moment. The mobile lay on the seat beside me, switched off, because I was driving, but I knew I would have to turn it on again soon so Mr Underworld could reach me. Or should I start calling him Mr Farr now that I was pretty certain who he was?

In the rear-view mirror I could still see the 'twins' enjoying themselves enormously at my expense. Thinking about Mr Underworld, I suddenly recalled how much useful information had come from the gossip of the ladies in Mum's salon. It was worth a try with these two.

'Do you two know a man named Farr, by any chance?'

'Parr?' asked Caroline.

'No, dear. Farr,' Deirdre corrected her.

'I'm certain she said Parr,' came the firm reply.

I groaned, then jumped in to stop them from enjoying themselves even further. 'Sorry, Caroline. I *did* say Farr. With an "F".'

They both looked disappointed that I'd interrupted their fun. 'Farr,' said Caroline slowly. 'Does he sell watches?'

'That's the one,' I said. 'Watches and jewellery.'

'Oh, yes. We both bought our watches from him,' Caroline continued. 'Nice man. Big family for this day and age. Three boys and two girls.'

'No, it's the other way round. Two boys and three girls.'

They were off again, but I was pleased that they knew him at least. I didn't take much notice of their remark that he was a nice man. To these two, anyone who smiled at them and let them argue for a few minutes would seem like a saint.

Meanwhile the old girls were getting serious in the back seat. 'I'm sure it's three girls,' said Deirdre. 'I know, because they're all at Cresswell House where Timothy sent his girls.'

I didn't have a clue who Timothy was, but I'd heard of Cresswell House. It was one of the most exclusive girls' schools in the city. 'What about the boys?' I asked. 'Where do they go to school?'

'Hudson Grammar. All three of them,' Caroline answered, emphasising the word 'three'. 'Though one of them is at university now. Wants to be a doctor.'

University! Doctor! All that would cost money and Hudson Grammar was *the* boys' school. 'It must cost a fortune to have your kids at those schools,' I commented.

They obviously hadn't thought about it in those terms. 'Nothing's too much to pay for a good education,' Deirdre said piously. Caroline nodded in agreement before she could stop herself.

I drove on, delighted that I had pumped these two

for gossip. Who needed police informers when there were treasure troves like the Eisenberg sisters around?

After my success with the Eisenbergs, I thought I'd try the same with some of my other clients. (It worried me a little that I now thought of them not only as clients, but as *mine*.) Janice was careful to avoid eye contact when I arrived to pick up the Duvals, and I suspected that she would have cancelled the trip if it had been up to her. But she couldn't afford to have Eric asking questions about why I might suddenly be out of favour.

Ha! Little did she know.

As it happened, they had something to say about Mr Farr the jeweller too, and there was no carry-on about his name this time. 'Oh, yes. We know him,' said Eric dismissively. 'Can't say that I've got much time for him.'

'Oh, why's that?' I asked with mock innocence.

'The man's a fool, that's why.'

I waited to see if he would offer any more, knowing that if I asked too much about Mr Farr they would want an explanation. Eric had said his piece, and I was afraid it sounded like a rather final statement. Then Janice came to the rescue.

'It's the woman he married who's the fool,' she added tartly. This was a new side of the Duvals I hadn't seen. They weren't quite the charming pair I had taken them for when I first drove them around. (And didn't I know that even better than they did themselves?) 'Ambitions beyond her station, if you ask me.'

'I heard they sent all their children to private schools,' I said. 'Must have cost a bomb.'

'That's only the half of it,' said Eric, re-entering the conversation. 'I used to have a beer with an old mate of mine up at the RSL. Gone now, poor bloke.' He turned to Janice. 'You remember Ern, don't you?' They chatted on about this dead acquaintance Ern, whoever he was, for quite a while, and I was becoming afraid Eric had forgotten why he had started on about him.

'What did Ern do?' I asked when their reminiscences finally petered out.

'Ern? Finance, of course. When he'd had a few, he'd tell me some home truths about the good citizens of Prestwidge. That young Farr, he was sailing close to the wind. He's never got the return from his jewellery shop that he was hoping for, and then he went and built that monstrosity up on the hill.'

'She *made* him build it, you mean. All flash and no substance, that woman.'

'Yes, well, that's what Ern told me years ago. The mortgage payments would bankrupt a small country. He must be in hock up to his gills.'

There it was. Bingo. (Well, in the circumstances, that's probably not the best expression!) But I now had Mr Farr pretty well pegged. He needed money, and perhaps he was just desperate enough to forge a copy of Narelle Sidebottom's ring to get some, and then to threaten Grandad and me when things went wrong.

What to wear, what to wear, what to wear …

Guys get it easy. They turn up in a clean pair of jeans, a shirt and a pair of lace-up shoes with their hair blowing in the wind and that's that. Of course, it's easier if they look like Chris Meagher to start with, but the principle remains the same for all of them.

It's girls who have it tough.

Pants. Definitely pants. The right thing to wear to a grotty pub like the Prestie Hotel. There was always the trusty standby, jeans. I tried on my newest pair and found they fitted the Sinclair shape perfectly. If anything, that last round of chocolate abuse had helped me fill them out to just the right measure of roundness. Chris turned up just as I was giving myself the final once over in the long mirror. Go, Rosie!

He came to the door this time. He was in denim again, with a matching jacket, worn with just the right degree of casual disdain. 'Hello, Mrs Sinclair,' he said, when Mum beat me to the front door, but he wasn't all over her like a rash, thank God. I could see her brain working. *How did my daughter score a hunk like this?* And she hadn't even seen his car!

Chris wasn't keen to hang around Mum (understandable), so we were out of there quickly and off to the red coupé. I stopped dead in my tracks. There was someone sitting in the passenger seat. He saw me pull up and chuckled to himself. 'I've got a little surprise for you.'

Yeah, well if he thought I was going out with his mates on some kind of double date, I had a surprise for *him*. I wasn't going through *that* a second time. Then he opened the door and the interior light came on.

'Oh, my God!' I squealed, sounding pathetic, I know, and so girlie, but what would any girl do if she was confronted by a huge teddy bear?

'It's the one from yesterday,' he told me, though there was no need. I'd recognise Teddy Christian anywhere.

'I went back to The Grove afterwards and found those old ladies. They argued a bit over the price ...'

'Don't tell me. They argued with *each other* over the price.'

'Yeah, how did you know?'

'Trust me, I know.'

Now I knew why the Eisenbergs had been smiling so wickedly from the back seat!

'I figured you'd like it. Go on, get in,' he said eagerly. 'I've got something else for you as well.'

Teddy Christian was placed proudly on my knee, as a stopgap until I could get his namesake in that position. No painful springs this time. He closed the door behind me and sauntered casually round to the other side. He knew I was desperate to find out what the second present was, and now he was teasing me. Once into his seat, he took a package from the dashboard above the steering wheel and passed it over. Whatever it was, it had been expertly wrapped in purple tissue paper and tied with a bright green bow.

The polite thing to do would have been to undo the bow and carefully unwrap the tissue paper to reveal the present inside. Forget all that crap. I ripped it open in one movement.

'My skirt! I don't believe it! It's the skirt I wore on Saturday night. How did …' This didn't make sense. How could he have got hold of it?

'It's not the same one, Rosie,' he laughed. 'It's a replacement. You mentioned where you'd bought it, remember? Rags for Ragers. I went there this afternoon.'

'But it's even my size!' I gasped, checking the label.

'Yeah, well, when I told them who it was for they remembered you. You were worried it made your bottom look too big or something.'

Yep, they'd remembered me.

'It doesn't, you know.'

'Doesn't what?'

He didn't embarrass me by repeating it. A wink was enough. He had a look on his face that I liked very much. He had redeemed himself completely in my eyes, and he knew it, though he made no effort to hide his arrogance. But what was one character flaw when he had so much else going for him?

'Look, Rosie, about my job. I can't tell you too much. I work for a few guys off and on, do a bit of security for classy parties in the city and that sort of thing. There's a world you don't see, a dangerous world, and people are willing to pay big-time for certain skills.'

I still had no idea what he did to pay for this car, but he had spoken with a sincerity that couldn't be faked. Some mysteries aren't for solving, I told myself. Just enjoy the ride.

We turned up at the pub to listen to the band. They were really good. They were really loud. I thought my ears would start bleeding. A few of the guys in the audience obviously knew Chris, nodding to him or holding up a beer to say cheers. The girls knew him too, all of them, and I could feel the daggers in my back. I could handle their bald-faced envy — to be honest, I kind of enjoyed it — but I couldn't ignore some of the comments that were slipped in deliberately, as sharp and wounding as any knife.

'Cradle snatcher' was one — aimed at Chris, not me, of course. He didn't hear it, but when the band finally stopped for a break one of the smart-arsed chicks asked me, 'How's school, then?' I swear, she had the gall to act like she was just making friendly conversation.

Chris fixed *her*. 'You didn't make it to Year Twelve, did you, Vanessa? I can still recall what Hoskins said about you in Year Nine. He had a real way with words, old Hoskins. Now, how did he put it?' Chris paused until he had everyone hanging on his next words. "More brains in a box of chalk than inside your head." That was it, wasn't it, fellas?'

'Half a box,' said one of his mates, as they all fell about laughing. 'He said "half a box" and he rattled the damn thing in front of her face, remember?'

Vanessa suddenly found she had to visit the ladies',

while a few other girls stopped laughing and started to squirm, terrified that Chris might dredge up their own scholastic underachievements. But he decided on a more direct route to make me part of the crowd. He came up close and put his arm around my shoulders, like I was one his drinking mates. 'You guys should have seen Rosie stick it to Enright the other day. Ran rings around him. She's got a real style of her own,' he assured them. 'Feisty and honest in a way that would leave you lot behind. "What you see is what you get", that's Rosie, and what you see is something special, eh,' he added.

Hearing this announced so bluntly by anyone other than Chris Meagher, I might have been insulted, but he had just the right look on his face to carry it off, and just the right tone in his voice to tease them but warn them at the same time.

Meanwhile, I was thinking about Glenda's motto, 'What you see is *all* you get', and wondering whether he understood that. Maybe Glenda was right. Maybe I was in a little over my head with this guy.

Oh, what the heck. I stopped worrying and got back to enjoying myself. Chris stayed at my side all night, the whole place was jumping, and we danced for hours in the middle of all that noise and smoke and the crush of bodies. I felt so alive, like I was plugged into a kind of electricity I'd never experienced before, a human buzz that thrilled my entire body.

We went home around midnight. Outside my place, we talked for a while, enjoying the vague sensation of numbed eardrums, and before I could stop it, my mind threw up a few things that Glenda and I had talked about.

Oh, boy.

I went quiet.

Chris went quiet.

Then he kissed me.

Oh, boy!

Fade to black.

TWENTY-FOUR

HEY, NOTHING HAPPENED! HONESTLY. CROSS my heart. (His red coupé has bucket seats, for God's sake!) But he didn't kiss me like I was his Aunt Rosie from the nursing home, either, trust me!

I woke to find someone named Christian sitting on the chair next to my bed looking ridiculously pleased with himself. It was the huge bear, of course, but I must admit that I was feeling ridiculously pleased with *myself* to see him there as a reminder of last night.

There were other reasons to feel pleased as well. I had pretty much worked out who had been ringing me up, demanding that ring back and making threats against my grandad along the way. Somehow, that made it all easier to deal with. The next time that sinister voice called me, I would simply arrange for the bad-tempered Kenny to pick up the ring and that would be the end of it. What did *I* care if Mr Farr had been trying to cheat some big-time businessman? It was Paddy Larkin I cared about. Maybe when Grandad was out of gaol, I'd tell him about Mr Farr and let *him* decide what to do.

I left the mobile on so the call could get through, since Mr Underworld (a.k.a. Mr Farr) had stopped leaving rude demands on my message bank. That's how Mrs Foat got hold of me. 'Rosie, I'm not too well. I'm in bed, actually.'

My heart raced. She might be a tough old boot, Mrs Foat, but with her sister dying a little more each day I couldn't bear the thought of her slipping away too.

She reassured me. 'It's nothing serious, but could you please pick up a prescription from the doctor's and have it filled for me?'

I was on my way. She did look pale when I arrived with her pills. She was sitting up in bed reading the paper without the least hint of self-pity. I took her a glass of water to help the handful of tablets down, then gave her some space while she swallowed them one at a time. More photos on the walls of her bedroom, I noticed — pictures of her family, all of them. There was a heart-warming portrait showing Mrs Foat and her husband surrounded by their children. It wasn't taken in a studio by a professional, but outside this very house on the patio by some fortunate amateur, a neighbour perhaps.

'Don't any of your children live nearby?' I asked, when I realised she was watching me.

'None,' she said. 'Vicky married a Frenchman.' Her tone told me what she thought of that. 'Lives in Toulouse. Heather moved interstate for her job a long time ago and she can only make it back for holidays. Not easy with a family.'

'What about your son?' I asked, looking more closely at the portrait. He was in his school uniform, all fresh-faced and anxious. Perhaps it was his first day at high school. There was no mistaking that daggy uniform; he was a Prestie, same as me. All this was going through my mind, so I missed her reply, but by then I was wondering about something else.

'Mrs Foat, do you still remember the names of your son's schoolfriends?'

'Oh, heavens, Rosie. I can't remember the names of my *own* schoolfriends.'

Oh, well, it was still worth a try. 'He didn't go to school with someone named Farr, did he?'

'Farr ...' She pondered this for a moment. 'You know, Rosie, I think he did.'

I couldn't believe my luck. I turned away from the picture and came closer. Mrs Foat's face had darkened and I knew something else was coming. 'You know why I remember, Rosie? There was an incident, at school, most unsavoury. Bullying.'

Unbelievable! I'd asked three lots of old wrinklies about Mr Farr and scored a hit every time. Was there anything about Prestwidge these old folk didn't know? Now she was going to tell me that Mr Farr was a bully at school. What better confirmation of my theory could I ask for?

I waited for Mrs Foat, but she seemed troubled — which was understandable, I suppose, if her son had been unhappy at school all those years ago. But she surprised me — turned the tables on me — in fact, she turned the tables upside down and dumped them on my head.

'It was my son who was the bully, I'm ashamed to say. He and his mates. Right little terrors, they were. They ganged up on that wretched Farr boy and made his life a misery.'

She paused a moment as though she were debating an important moral issue. 'Mind you, *no-one* had much time for him, timid little mouse that he was. A born victim, if you ask me — but we're not supposed to blame the victim these days, are we?'

Mrs Foat wasn't one to waste sympathy where she didn't think it was deserved. Despite the attempt to tell herself off, her deeply lined face broke into a traitorous smile. She leaned closer to me and whispered like a primary school girl with a shameful secret. 'Forgive my French, Rosie, but they used to call him "Jimmy Fart" and blow rude noises every time he walked by.'

This didn't fit in with my image of the horrible

Mr Farr at all. My good luck was crumbling around my ears, and the more she told me, the more I worried we might have the wrong guy. Hey, wait, I thought suddenly, maybe it's a different Farr we're talking about here. 'Do you know what happened to him, the boy named Farr? After he left school, I mean.'

'James Farr? Yes, I think so. He's still around in Prestwidge somewhere. A goldsmith or something like that.'

'A jeweller,' I moaned.

'Yes, that's it.'

I could simply ignore what Mrs Foat had told me. I mean, it was an option, wasn't it? Kids can change when they grow up. Timid little victims can grow up to be vicious wolves. (Yeah, and mice roar like lions.)

Who was I kidding? I could hear Glenda already. *Let's review the facts.* Time to go round and see her.

As soon as she opened the door, I could see she expected news of a different sort, though of course she would never ask, and would probably feign indifference anyway. 'Chris bought me a teddy,' I told her.

'He *what*! A teddy? One of those skimpy lingerie things?' She drew lurid lines on her body with her finger to show what she meant. 'I don't believe it! I'll break his kneecaps, the bastard.'

'Not that kind of teddy, you idiot.' I was allowed to call Glenda an idiot now and again. It sort of balanced out the number of times I was one for real.

I explained about the stuffed bear, which brought a snort of disdain. I offered to let her borrow it, because I knew she had a soft spot for big cuddly bears.

Then it was into a detailed account of last night: the bear again, the skirt and how he had come by it … I left out any bits I didn't think she should hear (like the interlude outside my house afterwards).

She wasn't about to let me get away with that. 'Drop the innocent schoolgirl act,' she demanded harshly. 'How far did you go?'

'Glenda! What sort of a question is that? All we did was kiss. His hands never left his arms. In fact, they remained visible at all times.' I mentioned the bucket seats, but she just rolled her eyes to show I had a lot to learn.

'Watch out, Rosie. He started out all sweet and cosy with me, too.'

She got off my case after this, giving me a chance to discuss my other problem. I told her what Mrs Foat had revealed about our prime suspect. 'I don't care what money troubles he's got, I just don't think someone who was a timid little boy and got bullied at school could threaten me the way this bloke's been doing. That voice is seriously nasty.'

'Maybe Jimmy Fart has hired a heavy to do his dirty work for him.'

'No, it was all very personal. The man I've been talking to definitely wants that ring for himself, and besides, there's that guy in the silver Commodore.

Kenny the muscle man, or whatever. Farr couldn't afford to hire the entire Mafia.'

We both thought about this in silence, knowing what had to be said but not wanting to be the one who said it. 'You know, Rosie, I've been thinking about your Mr Farr since yesterday and it doesn't quite make sense. Whether he's a wimp or not, it's still a huge risk he's taking. He couldn't sell the original ring as it was. Someone might recognise it.'

'He'd take the diamond out and sell it on its own.'

'Yes, but even so, what if the lovely Narelle suspected that she hadn't been given the same ring back, or it was strange in some way? She'd have it off to another jeweller straightaway and then the truth would be out. The cops would guess it had to be Farr and he'd be arrested and end up in gaol. He'd lose everything.'

'You're forgetting one thing, though. Mr Farr valued the ring at twenty thousand dollars and we know it's worth about four hundred. At the very least, he's lied about that.'

'True,' she conceded.

Great. We were back where we started, with more questions than answers and an unsolved mystery that could see my grandfather's fingers permanently shaped like question marks.

TWENTY-FIVE

THE PHONE RANG AND I jumped a foot off Glenda's
bed, but it was *her* phone so it couldn't be Mr
Underworld (now almost certainly NOT a.k.a. Mr
Farr). It was Mum, wanting to know if Glenda
would do a session at Hair by Sinclair that afternoon
so Mum herself could have a few hours off. Glenda
needed the money, so I said I'd drive her over to
the salon.

We were barely out of her street when the Mercedes
came alive with the dreaded trill of Grandad's mobile.
'Oh, God. It'll be him. He'll want to make final
arrangements for me to hand over the ring.'

I pulled the car over to the curb and took the

phone, still ringing, from Glenda's hand. 'What are you going to do?' she asked.

'Give it to him, I suppose. He'll go after Grandad if I don't.'

She nodded solemnly, but with the same air of defeat that I felt myself.

'Hello?'

'Rosie!' said a man's voice, far too cheerfully.

Well, at least it wasn't the voice I was expecting, though it wasn't one I was at all pleased to hear. 'Hi, Uncle Bruce. What can I do for you?'

'I'm just ringing to see how you're getting on.'

'Bullshit. You want to know whether I've found the ring.'

He didn't lose his cheery demeanour but he didn't deny my accusation either. 'Well, have you found it?'

'As a matter of fact, I have,' I told him, sick of the whole business. More than likely, I wouldn't have it by the end of the day in any case.

Bruce could barely hide his excitement. 'Thank God,' he said. 'That will get my dad off the hook at least.' Like he cares. 'Look, you'd better give it to me. I can make sure it gets into the right hands.'

'You don't know who's threatening Grandad any more than I do.'

'But I know the territory, Rosie. This needs an experienced hand.'

'NO,' I said sharply. 'Whoever he is, he's got *my* number, not yours. It will just confuse things if I give you the ring.'

He went on about how dangerous it was and how he knew how to handle himself. All bulldust, of course. He couldn't handle himself in a kindergarten. He wanted the ring for himself. Well, there was one sure way to stop him from wanting it any more. 'Uncle Bruce, the ring's a fake. It's only worth a few hundred dollars.'

'Don't make jokes, Rosie. It's been valued at twenty thousand dollars.'

'Yes, the original maybe, but the ring we found in the Mercedes is a copy.'

He still wanted to argue with me, but I soon fixed that when I told him how Glenda and I had visited a jeweller on the other side of town.

'You're spinning me a line.'

'No, it's true. We've got a jeweller's certificate and everything. Glenda's here beside me. I'll put her on.'

Glenda didn't look the least bit impressed by this offer. In fact, the sunny tan had left her face and she was busily criscrossing her hands in front of my eyes whispering, 'No way, no way.'

'I can't believe it. A fake,' Bruce murmured to himself. 'A copy.' He seemed to believe me now. 'But how?'

'It had to be Mr Farr.'

'Who?'

'The jeweller who was robbed. James Farr. For a while I thought it must be *him* on Grandad's mobile, trying to get the ring back so the police wouldn't find out, but I'm not so sure now. I mean, he must be involved somehow because he made the false valuation, but he'd have been taking a huge risk.'

'Risk ...' said Bruce down the phone to me. He was still stunned by what I had told him, still working it through.

'Yeah, if anyone had found out, the police would have been onto him straightaway.'

'The police would be the last of his worries. It's Terry Sidebottom he'd have to watch out for. If he's made a copy of that ring then he'd better make himself scarce, and fast, unless he wants ...' Even my uncle was reluctant to describe the punishment poor Mr Farr would suffer. 'Terry Sidebottom's a nasty piece of work,' he assured me with a hint of awe in his voice. 'He might be squeaky clean nowadays, but deep down ... well, a leopard can't change his spots, if you know what I mean.'

My mind dredged up images of bodies thrown into the river with concrete blocks around their ankles, shallow graves out in the bush somewhere, or cars plunging over a cliff edge.

Bruce went on. 'A fake, eh?' I could just see him scratching his stubbly chin. 'Then what happened to the original?' he murmured. But then his tone changed, as though it were a matter that wouldn't interest me. 'What are you going to do now, Rosie?'

'I don't know, Uncle Bruce. I just don't know.'

'Yeah, I can see that it's all a bit confusing for you. Well, good luck, eh!'

And that was it. I'd expected him to lose interest in the ring I'd found once he knew it was a fake, but to cut me off so abruptly was a new low even for Bruce Larkin.

I handed the phone to Glenda and headed the Merc towards Hair by Sinclair.

When we arrived on that Thursday afternoon, Tracey was doing Mum's nails and there wasn't another soul in the salon. 'Early afternoon,' my mother lamented. 'Can't get anyone to make an appointment for when the soaps are on TV.'

Glenda disappeared into the tiny staff area at the back, leaving me to slump into a chair beside the dog-eared, out-of-date magazines. The ring pressed uncomfortably through my jeans, making a painful indentation in my thigh. Fake or no fake, it was still hard and round and not exactly intended for pockets. Rings are supposed to be out on show, displayed on a woman's finger for all the world to see.

But I could hardly pull it out now, in front of Mum and Tracey. Like every other female in Prestwidge, they seemed to be intimately acquainted with Mrs Sidebottom's famous trophy. Did Mr Farr really think he was going to get away with it, pulling a scam involving such a notorious piece of jewellery? The timid, victimised Mr Farr. I almost felt sorry for him. But there it was again, the sense that I had it all wrong, that I was missing something obvious here.

'Mum. That ring, the one stolen from up on Gresham Street. You seem to know a lot about it, but have you ever seen it close up?'

Tracey made a squawking noise like a chicken stuck with a garden fork. 'Close up? Hard not to. It sort of lit the place up whenever she came in here.'

'Here? You mean you used to do Mrs Sidebottom's hair?'

'That was years ago,' said Mum. 'Now she goes to some limp-wristed *artiste* in the city.' She tried her best for a French accent on the word '*artiste*', and though she failed spectacularly to my ears, she had Tracey looking impressed. Tracey wouldn't know a Frenchman if he whacked her with the Eiffel Tower.

'I can't see what he can do that I can't.' My mother twiddled her fingers in an effort to dry her nail polish. Frankly, I could guess why anyone who had the dough would go elsewhere to have their hair done. One look at the way my mother wore her own hair would set the alarm bells clanging.

'So you saw the ring on her hand, then?'

'When something's stuck under your nose like a bit of rotten fish it's hard to ignore. It showed how far she'd gone up in the world, you see, and she never missed a chance to tell us all how it cost her husband an absolute bomb.'

'A symbol of his love,' I said, remembering the conversation we'd shared here a few days earlier. Mum recalled it too, and they both laughed, although Tracey hadn't even been here that day. But

I was feeling the pressure, and for a while, at least, my sense of humour had gone on holiday.

Even Mum noticed. 'Come on, Rosie. We laughed at her behind her back 'cause she was a stuck-up tart trying to convince us she was someone special. With that ring on her finger she could pretend in front of all of us but we knew that deep down she was just another Prestie.'

Tracey started on Mum's other hand. Glenda came out from the back room with a broom and began to sweep the hair out from beneath the chairs. There were a few rare moments of silence, until Tracey said, 'I'll tell you what though, I could never understand where Terry Sidebottom got the money.'

'What do you mean?' said Glenda, stopping mid-sweep. 'He's filthy rich, isn't he? Everyone says he's got money to burn.'

'Yeah, he's rolling in it now, but he wasn't back then, when he bought that ring for the lovely Narelle.'

'No, that's true,' Mum confirmed. 'I've never thought about it before, but you're right, Trace. He wasn't doing so well at the time, was he?'

I glanced up at Glenda, then at Mum. 'What are you saying? I thought he was a big-time crook.'

'Yes, but he had to divorce his first wife to marry the lovely Narelle, and the only way to get rid of her quickly was to give her whatever she asked for. The first Mrs S did very well out of the settlement, that's for sure. Lives high on the hog in the city somewhere, thanks very much.'

'I wish *my* first husband had been rich like that,' sighed Tracey, who was currently looking for her third, I think, or was it her fourth? (Another reason why Glenda and I hadn't wanted to end up as clones of Tracey.)

'When my husband took off, all he left was half a carton of beer,' said Mum. I was vaguely aware that she was talking about my father. 'I don't drink beer,' she added wistfully, as though she would have been satisfied with the deal if only it had been a bottle of gin instead.

'And then there was the problem with his business,' commented Tracey.

I was losing track. 'Dad didn't have a business,' I said. 'He drove a forklift.'

'Not your father's business,' moaned my mother, exasperated that she had raised a daughter who retained so little of the gossip she heard. 'I mean Terry Sidebottom's. He was a crook. *That* was his business,' she said.

'Sorry,' I said meekly. 'I remember now. The lovely Narelle made him sink all his money into real estate.'

'All except what it cost him for that ring,' Tracey pointed out.

'Yeah, well, she wasn't going to let him get away with something cheap, eh. The bigger the better. She had to have the flashiest ring he could afford, to stick under our noses.'

'He could have bought her something fake,' said a voice.

My head shot up. Two other heads swivelled round. It was Glenda who had spoken, her face filled half with mischief and half with amazement.

Her comment had certainly gobsmacked Mum and Tracey. It took them a moment to swallow and finally find their voices. 'Don't be ridiculous. He wouldn't have dared, not even a rogue like Terry Sidebottom. He knew how much that ring meant to the lovely Narelle. I told you ...'

'It was a symbol,' I said, cutting her off, but it was Mum who cut me off in return.

'Will you shut up about symbols, Rosie!' She turned to Tracey. 'I blame the school, honestly, I do. They were always going on about symbols and stuff when I was there. Didn't have a clue what they were talking about myself, but this one ...' She stabbed her thumb in my direction.

I didn't listen to the rest of her complaints. I was staring at Glenda, who was staring back at me. She wandered closer. 'Are you are thinking what I'm thinking?' she whispered.

I tapped the small bulge in my pocket. 'This isn't a copy. It's the real thing.'

'Only it's *not* real,' Glenda added.

I nodded towards the door then stood up to follow her out.

'Hey, where are you going, Glenda? Mrs Greatorex is coming in soon.'

'I won't keep her long,' I assured Mum. 'There's something we have to talk over.'

TWENTY-SIX

'I DON'T BELIEVE IT,' SAID Glenda.

'You were the one who suggested the stone wasn't real in the first place,' I pointed out. 'And you have to agree, it makes sense.'

We had crossed the road to Josie's Coffee Lounge, where we slumped heavily onto two chairs at the corner table.

'But for her to wear that ring all these years and not know the stone was fake ...' said Glenda, flabbergasted.

'She never had a reason to be suspicious. I mean, who's going to know the difference around here? And from what I've heard about the lovely Narelle, no-one was going to ask her to prove her precious diamond was real. She's even nastier than her husband. She'd rip your tongue out and shove it in your ear.'

'So you think that Mr Sidebottom had the ring made with a fake diamond in the first place?'

I nodded. 'He needed every penny left over from the divorce to set up his property business. He just didn't have the money for a flashy diamond, not one the size of California, anyway. And if Mrs Sidebottom hadn't caught her hand in the car door, it would still be his guilty secret.'

'So Mr Farr is mixed up in this by mistake, all because of a little accident.'

'Yes, poor Jimmy Fart. He might be a wimp, but he *is* a proper jeweller. He must have known the diamond was fake as soon as he saw it.'

I sat there imagining the scene: Mrs Sidebottom, the lovely Narelle who scares the pants off every man in Prestwidge (including her husband), standing at the counter in front of timid Mr Farr. She was probably full as a fowl after a long lunch with her girlfriends, and on top of that she would have been upset over her ring. 'He must have been shitting bricks,' I muttered aloud.

'Concrete blocks,' said Glenda, making shapes with her hands, which I hoped weren't meant to be as rude as they looked. 'Jeez, *I* wouldn't have told her,' she said.

'Neither would I,' I added, unashamed of my cowardly tone. 'If I were Mr Farr, I'd have fixed the ring as fast as I could and hoped I never saw it, or her, again.'

'Hey, wait a minute, what about the valuation?' Glenda pointed out. 'He signed a certificate, like the one I got from that other jeweller. He said it was worth twenty thousand dollars. He didn't have to do that. He could have just fixed the broken claws and washed his hands of it.'

'Good point. He has to be in on this scam somehow. I just can't see him doing it on his own.'

'Someone threatened him, you mean?'

'It would be easy enough — a timid little loser like Mr Farr. And he's got money worries of his own,' I added, remembering my conversation with the Duvals.

Things had been spiralling about in my head as I went over everything I'd found out in the past few days. Odd ideas clashed together, contradicting each other, and then a certain word or a phrase would jump out, demanding that I take a closer look.

One of those phrases had come from Uncle Bruce. *A leopard can't change his spots.* I thought about the leopard Uncle Bruce had been referring to.

'Glenda, the man who's been threatening me on the mobile,' I said cautiously, my tone making her sit up and wait for my next pronouncement. 'He knows the stone in that ring isn't real, right?'

She nodded, eyeing me uneasily.

'And we're pretty sure it's not Little Jimmy Fart.'

More nodding.

'Then it has to be someone else who knows the rings is a con job, and the only other person ...'

Glenda's eyes were suddenly round and wide like a pair of dinner plates. '... is Terry Sidebottom himself!' she gasped, loud enough for the rest of Prestwidge to hear. 'He *must* know, because he had it made in the first place!'

'Yes, and for all these years he's got away with it. Then he gets home from the office one night and the lovely Narelle informs him she's damaged the famous ring, but tells him not to worry because she's put it in at the jeweller's to be fixed.

'He must be having kittens at this point. He knows damn well the jeweller will realise the stone's a fake, and he's scared shitless that the lovely Narelle will find out.'

'She'd go ballistic,' said Glenda, racing ahead of me as always. 'God, think of it. Everyone in Prestwidge would know the famous engagement ring was a fraud. The rock she's flashed around the neighbourhood for years to put us all in our place ... it's an imitation! She'd be a laughing stock, wouldn't be able to show her face on the street for a hundred years at least.'

'She'd divorce him just to get back a bit of self-respect!'

'*Divorce?*' squawked Glenda, again letting the entire neighbourhood into our supposedly discreet conversation. 'Rosie, she'd take every cent he had!'

So it made sense that Terry Sidebottom, pillar of the community and devoted husband, would scoot down to Mr Farr's jewellery store and start throwing his weight around like the crook he used to be.

Glenda tried her hand at guessing the rest. 'And you think Terry Sidebottom made Farr sign that valuation?'

'That way, he's covered with the lovely Narelle. It's beautiful,' I added, in admiration at the guy's audacity. 'And I bet it's not the first time he's browbeaten some poor jeweller into giving a false valuation — Narelle would have expected the ring to be insured for a packet, wouldn't she? All part of acting superior. Then she could brag to everyone that her husband pays out more for insurance each year than other husbands spend on a ring in the first place.'

'Jeez, he was unlucky, then,' said Glenda thoughtfully. 'Of all the jewellery stores in the world, that dill decides to knock over Mr Farr's.'

I didn't make any reply when she said this. The silence stretched on and Glenda began to shuffle uncomfortably in her seat. 'What's up?' she asked finally. 'You've got a funny look on your face.'

'It's a little too much of a coincidence, don't you think?'

'You mean the robbery?' She stopped to think about this, leaving me to watch the ideas fall into place behind her eyes like a winning spin on a slot machine. 'You think it was a set-up!'

'Well, put yourself in Terry Sidebottom's place.' I was spending a lot of time trying to think like a crook. What's more, I'd found I was good at it! 'Here's the perfect chance to get himself off the hook, permanently. He makes Farr do a phoney valuation and then has the ring stolen in a burglary he arranges himself. So long as the ring never turns up, the insurance company has to pay out, and he can let his wife pick out a new ring, with a real stone this time. It's brilliant! Only a criminal mind could see the opportunity.' (And mine, of course. I *was* Paddy Larkin's granddaughter, after all.)

'What do you mean, "pick out a ring"?' said Glenda scathingly. 'This is the lovely Narelle we're talking about. She'd have a ring *specially made*, even bigger and flashier than the first one.'

'And she'd make sure she spent every last cent of the insurance money, too, just as a matter of principle. There's no way Terry would get his hands on *any* of that dodgy twenty grand.'

Glenda was doing her best to keep up with me. 'No wonder Sidebottom wants the ring himself. If the police end up with it, they'll soon find out it's a phoney and then the whole scam will blow up in his face.' Finally she focused on me solemnly. 'Are you going to take the ring to the police after all?'

'I can't,' I told her. 'It's not that I give a damn about Terry Sidebottom, or Mr Farr — or anything that happens to this stupid ring,' I added, patting my pocket. 'It's Grandad.'

There was no need to explain. But Glenda was Glenda, university student by day and exotic dancer by night. Both of these pursuits encouraged a healthy scepticism. 'Can you be sure you're right about Terry Sidebottom?'

In all honesty, I could only shake my head.

'In that case, we'd better get some proof,' she announced.

'How?'

'Easy. You think the voice on your mobile is Terry Sidebottom, right? You'd recognise it if you heard it again, wouldn't you?'

I nodded uncertainly.

'Right, then. We'll ring him.'

'What do you mean, "We'll ring him"?'

'He's in the phone book, isn't he?'

'He'll be at work!'

'We'll ring him there, then,' responded Glenda casually. 'Look, *Prestwidge Land & Housing*.' She read from a *For Sale* sign in the window of the shop next door to Hair by Sinclair. 'And the number's underneath. We don't even *need* a phone book.'

'So what do we do? Ring him up and say, "Hi, Mr Sidebottom! It's Rosie Sinclair speaking. I've been meaning to ask, are you the guy who's been threatening me and my grandad because your plan to cheat your insurance company has ended up in the toilet?"'

'No need to be sarcastic, Rosie,' she scolded me. 'You just need to listen to his voice for long enough to work out whether it's him or not.'

'He'll recognise my voice first, though.'

'Mmmm, you're right …' Glenda hadn't thought of that. 'I'll have to do it for you, then.'

I was glad *she* felt brave enough, because *I* certainly didn't. It was bad enough when *he* rang *me* (if it *was* him), but for *me* to ring *him* …

'But if it's you on the phone, how will I hear his voice well enough to know one way or the other?'

Another good question that Glenda hadn't managed to answer yet. It didn't take long to find a solution, however. 'The salon!' she exclaimed as we stood up from the table. 'Your mother put in an extension, didn't she?'

Glenda was right. The gossip didn't just arrive at Hair by Sinclair in the form of talkative clients. Women were ringing up all day long to tell Mum and Tracey things, so if it was a slack time, like this afternoon, Mum would get on the phone at the front desk and Tracey would listen in on the extension in the back room.

Mum was ready to leave when we arrived back from the café. She didn't look half bad for a forty-three year old. Freshly groomed nails and hair (Tracey had done that too, no doubt, but it could have been worse), and the outfit was new, not what she usually wore to work. I stopped dead in my tracks. She wasn't taking after the Duvals was she? The idea was too disgusting to contemplate — even *worse* than thinking about the Duvals. I shuddered and let the thought lapse quickly into the *Don't Want to Go There* compartment of my fevered brain.

'See you at home later, Rosie,' she called, waving.

Mrs Greatorex had arrived and was meekly submitting to a shampoo and rinse while Tracey told her the latest. (At Hair by Sinclair, only half the money you paid was for the haircut. The rest was for the gossip.)

Glenda was already at the front desk with the phone in her hand, waiting until I was almost into the back room before she dialled. I watched her stab the numbers into the keypad before picking up the receiver.

'... & Housing. Lisa speaking. How can I help you?'

'I'd like to speak to Mr Sidebottom, please,' said Glenda's voice, sounding as though she were at least thirty.

Lisa's voice became a little less light-hearted. 'May I ask who is calling?'

There was just the slightest hesitation, which I doubt the girl noticed, though I did. Glenda was thinking of a name. 'Witherspoon,' she said.

I nearly gave the game away with a choking noise into the extension. Reese Witherspoon was Glenda's favourite Hollywood star. But then, everyone had heard of her, hadn't they?' Please don't say 'Reese', I begged her silently.

'Er, Jane Witherspoon,' said Glenda quickly, and I relaxed. Lisa didn't suspect a thing.

'And may I ask the nature of your business?'

Glenda hadn't expected to be held up like this, I could tell. 'Does it matter?' she asked bluntly. 'I just need to speak to him.'

'Mr Sidebottom is a busy man. Unless this is an important matter it might be better for me to take your number and have him ...'

'No, it's vital I speak to him now. I'm calling on behalf of ...' Again, the slightest hesitation, then, '... of Clayton, Banks and Coffee, Solicitors-at-Law.'

Solicitors-at-Law! Go, Glenda! I knew immediately how she had come up with the name, too. Side by side, over the road from the salon, were Clayton's Menswear, the National Bank and Josie's Coffee Lounge, where we had just been. The name, the official language, everything. Surely it would impress the posh little knickers off Miss Lisa.

Well, not quite. 'And your call is in relation to ...?'

'I'm not at liberty to divulge the subject matter, except to Mr Sidebottom himself.'

That was uni for you. I mean, was that high-powered or what? I was lucky to have Glenda in there batting for me. The stony-voiced Lisa finally gave in. 'I'll put you through now.'

Oh, boy, here we go, I thought. The next voice I'll hear will be Terry Sidebottom's. 'Hello? Ms Witherspoon, is it. What can I do for you?'

The voice was pleasant, but a little wary. He must have been warned by his secretary that this was something big and he was taking the cautious route. It didn't help me at all. His voice *could* be Mr Underworld, but the tone was all wrong.

'Oh, er, Mr Sidebottom,' stammered Glenda. I realised that she was suddenly overwhelmed. She had put so much effort into bluffing her way past snooty Miss Lisa that now she was lost for words. 'Um, thank you for taking my call, Sir. I work for — at least, I represent ...' She was trying hard to use the kind of words lawyers use, but she couldn't quite manage the same mildly arrogant manner that they squeeze into every word. Worse still, she seemed to have forgotten whom she did work for. Hardly surprising when they didn't exist!

'Clayton, Banks and Coffee,' said Mr Sidebottom. Miss Lisa must have phoned through the name. At least *someone* remembered. 'I haven't heard of your firm before. Is this in relation to a property matter?'

'Property matter. Oh, yes, actually it is.' Glenda was losing it rapidly.

'Well?' said Mr Sidebottom, a little irritably. When Glenda didn't speak immediately, he jumped in again. 'Listen, Ms Witherspoon. I am happy to speak to you, since you told my secretary that this is an important matter. But would you please state your business.'

'My business. Oh, yes, well. One of our clients ...'

'*Which* client?' snapped Mr Sidebottom. 'If you would just give me a name, then I could at least get some idea of what this matter is about.'

I didn't hear the rest of the conversation, because I had already put down the phone. I hurried out to the front desk, and by the time I arrived I could heard an irate voice shouting into my best friend's ear. I stabbed down on the button, ending the call, and took the phone from a dazed-looking Glenda.

'I'm sorry,' she said. 'I didn't know what to say and then he got stroppy.'

'That was just what I needed!' I reassured her, resting my hand gently on her shoulder. 'I couldn't tell it was him until he started to go off at you.'

'So it *was* him? It was the same voice you've been hearing on the mobile?'

My face must have shown an odd mixture of a smile and the grim anxiety I felt throughout every part of my body. 'Certainly was,' I said. 'Terry Sidebottom is definitely our man.'

We suddenly became aware of our strangely silent surroundings, and turned around to find both Tracey and Mrs Greatorex staring at us like a pair of wide-eyed antelopes. Before we could invent even the smallest lie as an explanation, the mobile rang.

It could be Mrs Foat wanting a lift to the hospital. It could be the Duvals wanting something from the shop, or the Eisenberg sisters, who just wanted me to listen to their arguments. Yes, it could be any of them, but I had a sinking suspicion who it would be.

'Hello?'

'Rosie.'

Yep. Mr Underworld himself (a.k.a. Mr Sidebottom — and that was something we knew for certain, at last). I didn't say a word.

'Rosie? Answer me, you little bitch.'

Ooh, nasty. But no way was I making a sound.

He was no fool. He'd guessed what the call from Ms Witherspoon was about. I punched at the End button, the second time in a minute that I'd cut off a call in this way. I knew as I did so that I was also starting a stopwatch. Terry Sidebottom knew I knew, and he would have his young mate Kenny out after me in no time flat.

The clock was ticking.

'He knows you know,' said Glenda.

'I know he knows I know.'

'What are we going to do?'

'I don't know.'

This wasn't a very promising conversation. 'The most important thing is to make sure Grandad's OK. Maybe I'll just leave the mobile switched on and wait for Sidebottom to call back. We can make arrangements and this time I *will* hand over the ring.'

'Rosie, he won't be patient any more now. Not if he knows ...'

I put my hand up to stop her from doing the whole 'He knows you know' thing again.

We had stepped outside the salon for this little chat so that Tracey wouldn't add it all to her store of gossip. God knows what Mum was going to say when Tracey told her what she had heard already. I would worry about that some other time.

Two women approached along the footpath, one from each direction. They reached the door into the salon at the same moment, and after smiling briefly at Glenda and me, they went inside.

'I'd better get going,' I said.

'Where?'

Good question.

'I'll come with you,' said my best friend.

'No, you've got clients waiting. Maybe I'll go up to Pine Street and get Chris Meagher to help me.'

'I'm *definitely* coming with you, then.'

I managed to talk her out of it but as I slipped behind the wheel of the Mercedes I realised I might as well paint a target on the doors. They wouldn't have to look hard to find me. Should I do what I'd said to Glenda, and ask Chris for help?

No, I decided. I was probably overdramatising things, anyway. The simplest and safest thing to do was just to give up the ring. Nobody would get hurt then, not Grandad and not me. I hoped so, anyway. I mean, even a guy like Terry Sidebottom wouldn't resort to murder, would he?

This was definitely one for the *Don't Want to Go There* compartment. I let the old Mercedes drive itself for a while until I'd calmed down. That was better. My heart rate dropped back below two hundred beats per minute. The trouble was, it raced up again as soon as I thought about that mongrel getting away with his clever scam.

Maybe I *should* go to the police after all. I could ask them to give Paddy Larkin special protection in gaol, but that thought didn't fill me with much confidence. 'Never trust the cops.' Paddy himself was always telling us that. 'They'll promise you anything until they get what they want, and as soon as they've got it you're on your own.' I couldn't afford to let that happen to Grandad.

Besides, Terry Sidebottom would slither out from under me anyway. He could always claim the ring in my pocket was a copy and the original was still missing. No, going to the police was too risky. I wished there was something that could frighten Mr Sidebottom just enough for him to leave me and Grandad alone.

I drove on, not having a clue where I was going, checking the rear-view mirror every few seconds.

Wow. Suddenly it hit me like a ram raid. That was *it*! It wasn't some*thing* that frightened Terry Sidebottom. It was some*one*.

TWENTY-SEVEN

I PULLED OVER AND RANG Directory Assistance. A minute later, the phone was ringing in the Sidebottoms' home, wherever that was.

'Mrs Sidebottom?'

'Mum's down at The Grove,' said a boy probably about twelve years old.

No good going to her home, then. I had to make sure the ring was delivered right into her manicured hand. What to do? I started up the Mercedes again and headed towards The Promenade. My plan was to find Mrs S and somehow give her the ring. Details were hazy at this stage, but at least I knew what she looked like. She and Terry appeared together smiling in the local rag so many times they could have been politicians.

I was well along The Promenade, with less than a kilometre to go before I reached The Grove, when I saw the silver Commodore three cars back. It couldn't do much for the moment, though, with so much traffic around (and so many witnesses). I flew into the car park under Prestwidge Grove, scraping the bottom of the Merc on the speed bump along the way. Couldn't let Kenny catch me now.

Luck was with me. God, I love old people. There was an ancient sedan in front of the Commodore, and no-one was going to make the equally ancient gentleman behind the wheel rush his search for a parking spot. I shot ahead down the row and poked the Merc into the first space I could find, a disabled parking spot again. (Sorry!) Then I hotfooted it upstairs into the shopping precinct.

OK, so I'd ditched the transport, but the chase remained much the same. How was I going to find the lovely Narelle while at the same time remaining invisible to the not-so-lovely Kenny?

I spotted Kenny as he ran up from the car park, and once he had set out in one direction I ducked away in the other, down one of the wide walkways. There was no sign of Mrs Sidebottom. This was nerve-racking stuff.

Think, Rosie. Now, where could she be? I used my feminine instincts. There was only one dress shop in The Grove that could possibly call itself a boutique, and that's where I headed. To my complete and utter surprise, my luck stayed strong. There she was, standing proudly in full view of anyone passing by, as the assistant held up dress after hideous dress against her.

There she is, Rosie, I told myself, the woman you've been chasing. Time to get on with it. I felt the ring digging into my thigh still. Would I be glad to get rid of it, or what?

I sauntered into the boutique as casually as I could under the circumstances, but unfortunately this was the kind of place where you weren't allowed to browse alone. A sales assistant descended upon me the way a vulture descends on a dead zebra.

'Hello, I'm Amanda. Are you looking for anything special?' She looked more like a Mandy to me. A Prestie dressed up like something she wasn't. Look at those fake eyelashes. She could sweep the floor with them. Did she really think classy women had to try so hard? I didn't care much whether Mandy bunged on an act for my benefit, but the trouble was that she drew the attention of Mrs Sidebottom and her assistant as well. She didn't recognise me, of course, because there was no reason why she should, but what was I going to do now? Bounce over, pull the ring out of my pocket and ask her if she had dropped it?

I was a total fool. Had I really expected just to give back the ring and walk away? She would want to know who I was, and what I was doing with her ring, then she would start screeching for the police, and before I knew it I'd be in a cell down at the station waiting for Mum to bail me out.

Face it, Rosie, I confronted myself. This is never going to work.

I told Amanda I had changed my mind and fled into the crowd who were traipsing zombie-like towards the circular hub of The Grove. At the absolute centre of this hub was a small information counter with a lone woman attending it. I stood watching her aimlessly, hoping for inspiration, when she picked up a microphone and flicked a switch on the desk in front of her. Immediately there was a faint snap from a speaker high above us.

'Good afternoon, shoppers.' It was the soothing sound of everyone's sweet-natured Auntie Gladys, and completely innocuous. 'We have a little boy here who has lost his mummy. His name is Jacob, and he is waiting for her at the information counter in the centre of Prestwidge Grove. Thank you.' Snap. End of announcement.

The woman stooped and offered a lolly to the mop-top of little Jacob's head, which I could just make out behind the counter. Oh, well, that's one bit of lost property that will definitely find its owner today.

So I'm slow. I admit it. I had turned away and headed back to the car park before I realised the significance of what I had just witnessed. In fact, after checking carefully to make sure Kenny wasn't lying in wait, I had already unlocked the Mercedes when it hit me. *Lost property!* What was I carrying uncomfortably in my jeans but twenty thousand dollars' worth of lost property? (Four hundred dollars' worth if you wanted to get technical.)

This time I took a moment to think it through. How would I do it? I wish I planned my love life so thoroughly. I realised I needed a disguise, and though it seemed ridiculous, I knew I had one ready to hand. I opened the glove box and took out Glenda's black wig, and her sunglasses, which were still there too. I put them both on and looked at myself in the rear-view mirror. She'd managed to look like Uma Thurman; I looked like Bonzo the Clown.

I needed to improvise a bit more. What else was in the car? I looked around, but since I had to keep the back seat tidy out of respect for my elderly passengers, there was nothing useful to be found there. After another check for Kenny, I opened the boot and found a Rags for Ragers bag, which contained Glenda's knock-'em-dead little skirt. It would have to do.

I kept the wig, the sunglasses and the skirt in the bag until I had bought an envelope and a cheap pen at the newsagent. Then it was into the toilets, where I shimmied out of my jeans and into the black skirt and tried my best with the wig. Oh God, don't look in the mirror, I told myself. The first guy to see me will probably ask how much! It wasn't exactly the kind of disguise that let me go unnoticed, but at least the sunglasses gave me a feeling of being someone else.

I took a deep breath and pushed my way out of the ladies', drawing either a gobsmacked stare or a disapproving frown from every person I passed.

There was the information counter.

I turned away.

No, I had to do it.

I turned back.

'Excuse me,' I said, to attract the woman's attention. Once she set eyes on me I certainly had her attention. 'I found this envelope in the ladies'. It must have fallen out of someone's handbag. I thought I'd better hand it in as lost property.'

The woman didn't know quite what to make of *me*, but my request was simple enough.

'It has someone's name on it, see? *Narelle Sidebottom*. Perhaps you could page her to see if she's still in The Grove.'

Now I was telling her how to do her job, but she still seemed determined to play the sweet auntie roll. 'Thank you. That's very kind of you to hand it in.'

'Just doing the right thing,' I said, brushing away the page-boy bob that dangled around my cheeks.

Then I was outta there fast. Oops, there was Kenny heading my way. He might not recognise me in the wig and sunglasses, but as I knew all too well, my disguise sort of shouted 'Disguise!', and he wasn't so thick that he wouldn't work out it could be me. I slipped into a computer game shop and watched him hurry past. Phew!

261

Before I could work up the courage for a dash to the car park, the announcement came over the speaker. 'Good afternoon, shoppers. Would Narelle Sidebottom please call at the information desk. That's Narelle Sidebottom to the information desk. Thank you.' Click.

I could just see the information desk through the window of the computer game store. It seemed safe here, and I knew I wouldn't feel the job was done until I saw with my own eyes that the lovely Narelle had been reunited with her gaudy ring. I could risk it, surely.

Three minutes passed, then five, and at last I realised I had been standing there almost ten minutes. No sign of Mrs Sidebottom. Had she gone home before the announcement was made? I waited. And waited. Still no-one came to collect the envelope. It had all been for nothing!

'Rosie?'

Oh, shit! Who's that?

I turned and found a rather bewildered Todd Rooney staring at me. 'It is you, isn't it, under that wig?'

It was bad enough that I had been caught in the silly disguise. To deny it would only make matters worse. 'Yes, it's me,' I said. I pulled the stupid wig from my head and took off the sunglasses, quickly stepping away from the window in case Kenny came back this way.

'What's with the wig? Makes you look like Uma

Thurman in *Pulp Fiction*.' No it didn't, but it was nice of him to say so. He didn't know whether to laugh or take the whole thing seriously. Neither did I.

'Just a practical joke,' I said pathetically. 'Too hard to explain. Look, Todd, I can't really hang around and talk. I've got a few things to do. How about I ring you when I get home tonight?'

Poor guy. He seemed so friendly, when really he had every right to be extremely rude to me after I lied to him about last Saturday night. Now he looked positively stricken, like I'd told him he stank or something. I felt awful. But at the same time, I started backing out of the store, ready to run.

Too late. I looked along the wide, fake marble passageway and there was Kenny, already increasing his pace and heading straight towards me. I took off, though where I would find refuge I had no idea. A huge department store lay ahead, and without any obvious alternative, I hurried in among the counters and displays, totally oblivious to the racks and aisles around me.

But wait, I was in some kind of clothing department, and if it was a clothing department then it would have change rooms. I took a closer look around. Lingerie everywhere — knickers, bras, nighties. Even teddies, which made me think of Glenda. There were the change rooms against the back wall. Before Kenny could reach me I pulled aside the curtain in front of the first one I came to, hoping desperately that it was empty.

It was! I was safe, for now. He wouldn't dare follow me through the curtain, surely. Or at least I hoped he wouldn't. I mean, guys aren't supposed to hang around in a place like this, are they?

Kenny obviously hadn't read the rules, because he barged straight in and stood right outside my cubicle.

'Give me the ring,' he whispered through the curtain.

I pretended not to hear him, but apart from that I was all out of ideas. I had no doubt that any second Kenny would simply brush aside the curtain and step into the cubicle with me.

Then there was a voice. 'May I help you, Sir?'

'Oh, er, no. It's OK. I'm just waiting while my girlfriend tries something on.' He wasn't completely thick, then.

'I see,' said the woman somewhat sternly. 'Perhaps you would like to stand back a little. There are other ladies in adjacent cubicles. I'm sure you understand.'

I heard his footsteps back away, then the woman called out to me. 'May I be of assistance, Miss?'

I pulled the curtain back a little and motioned for her to come inside. She took one look at me in the little black number and rolled her eyes with withering contempt. I have a big thing about shop assistants who think they are God's gift, but this wasn't the time to take up the crusade.

'That guy's not my boyfriend at all,' I whispered. 'He's a perv. Been watching me for the last ten minutes. I came in here to get away from him. Could you call security or something?'

The woman's nostrils flared. She was about my height but immaculately dressed: crisp creases in her starched white blouse, well-cut skirt to the knee. Her hair didn't show a strand out of place (Mum would have called the look 'severe') and the make-up was just right, nothing overstated but enough to accentuate her high cheekbones and cupid's-bow lips. Unlike 'Amanda', this woman was the real deal. What she was doing working in Prestwidge I just can't imagine. 'Security? Oh, that won't be necessary,' she told me coldly.

She doesn't believe me! She thinks I'm a tart playing games and making a nuisance of myself! 'But it's true!' I insisted.

'Wait here, please, Miss,' she advised, but as she backed out of the cubicle, pulling the curtain into place with a snap of her wrist, I detected an odd kind of excitement on her face. What had I come across here?

I was about to find out.

'Excuse me, Sir,' she said, apparently heading straight for Kenny. I risked a peek around the edge of the curtain just in time to see her march straight up to my pursuer. 'The young lady says you're not her boyfriend but some kind of voyeur who's been stalking her.'

'That's ridiculous! I don't know what you're talking about.'

'I'm sorry, Sir, but I must ask you to accompany me to the Manager's office.'

'I'm not going anywhere.'

Exactly what happened next is a bit of a blur, to tell you the truth, mainly because the perfectly groomed shop assistant moved like lightning. Kenny moved too, though his movements were not what he intended. They involved his feet temporarily appearing where his head had been, followed by a dull thud. When I dared to venture from the safety of the cubicle and join the small crowd that had gathered, I found Kenny eating carpet while the unruffled sales assistant pulled his arm painfully up behind his back. He struggled briefly, but she discouraged this activity by stamping down rather firmly on his shoulder blade with the ball of her foot.

I didn't stay to see how it ended. Instead I went on the prowl for the lovely Narelle.

TWENTY-EIGHT

NO SIGN OF HER. I searched for ten minutes, unable to decide whether it was better to move around, hoping to spot her, or wait in one place until she came past. Of course, Kenny might talk his way out of the Manager's office and come looking for me again, but somehow I thought my saviour from the lingerie department had lengthy plans for him. I was pretty sure I could afford to take my time.

The announcement went out again over the loudspeaker, the auntie voice slightly firmer this time. 'Would Narelle Sidebottom please report to the information desk.'

I headed towards the centre of The Grove, and who did I find keeping pace with me but the lady herself. Her stride was as determined as mine, so there seemed no doubt she had heard the announcement this time. I forced myself to keep staring straight ahead, then veered away from her until I reached a spot where I could watch her unobserved.

There she was at the information counter. I could just imagine the words.

I'm Narelle Sidebottom. There was an announcement.

Yes, Madam. This envelope has been handed in. It has your name on it.

The woman with the kindly aunt's voice gave her the envelope. She stared down at it, bewildered for a moment, frowned, hesitated, then as she realised there was something inside, something of a certain shape and size, her hands ripped at the paper feverishly. Then a scream, or more a squeal really. Whatever it was, it attracted the attention of everyone who heard it.

'*My ring! My ring!*' cried the lovely Narelle, over and over. I could hear that part clearly. There were tears aplenty and little jumps for joy, which, considering the flimsy stilettos she was wearing, might easily have brought her to grief. She slipped the ring immediately onto her finger as inquisitive fellow shoppers gathered round. '*My ring! Oh, my ring! I never thought I'd see it again!*'

It wasn't long before the questions started flying. *Who had handed in the envelope? Where was she now? Did she leave a name?* It was time for me to disappear, but as I turned to flee the scene, I found myself staring into the same perplexed face for the second time in ten minutes.

'What's going on?' asked Todd Rooney. He looked over my shoulder towards the pandemonium. 'You've got something to do with all that, haven't you?'

I had to get away. The wig and sunglasses were out of sight in the plastic bag, but the silly skirt might still give me away. 'No,' I said to Todd, already on the move. 'I don't know what you're talking about.'

This time, though, Todd didn't stay rooted to the spot. He fell into stride with me as I headed for the ramp leading to the car park below. 'Then why the wig? You have got something to do with it, haven't you?'

We were starting to attract attention. 'Yes, all right, it's true, but it's a long story.'

'Are you going to tell me?'

I looked over my shoulder. We were out of sight of the information desk now, but I didn't want to take any chances by hanging around with Todd. I looked at him, and into those gorgeous eyes, so innocent and appealing. 'Do you want a ride home?' I asked.

'Sure, as long as I get an explanation along with the ride.'

'OK, OK! Let's go!'

I thought I could tell Todd just a little of what had happened in the last week or two, enough for him to understand why I had been wearing a ridiculous wig and acting so strangely at The Grove. But it didn't work out that way at all. One piece of information would link up with another and I would have to reveal that tiny bit more, or else a single fact simply wouldn't make sense to Todd. Before I knew it, I'd told him the whole story.

'I don't suppose that guy I saw you with on Saturday was part of this?'

'Well, sort of. I couldn't tell you about it at the time ... but he had some information I needed, and ... and ... he would only let me have it if I went out with him.'

What a shameless pack of lies! I was definitely going to hell now. It was the way he was looking at me that had made me say that. Even though I had embarrassed him, let him down, been cruel to him, deceived him he still seemed to like me, and to be honest, I still liked him. Besides, I didn't seem to be thinking straight by that time. My entire body had began to shake, as though the successful return of Mrs Sidebottom's ring had released all the anxiety I had kept under wraps for days now. I had to drive at a snail's pace just to keep control of the car.

'Are you all right, Rosie?' Todd asked with genuine concern when we pulled up outside his house. 'You're shivering.' He put his hand gently on my arm. 'You're sweating, too.'

I was? Oh, God, he was right.

'Why don't you come in for a drink?'

He came round and opened the driver's door for me, and like a zombie, I slipped out and let him lead me inside like I was a motherless lamb. There was no-one else at home, it seemed, and before I knew it, we were sitting in director's chairs on his back verandah, with glasses of icy-cold soft drink in our hands.

I was still trembling, and I had realised why. 'He's going to call again, you know.'

'Who?' asked Todd.

'Mr Sidebottom. It's not over yet. I know he's going to call and yell at me and make all sorts of threats against my grandad. That's why I'm so nervous.'

It was true. I had returned the ring to its rightful owner without going to the police and I had foiled all of the dreadful Mr Sidebottom's plans. But the danger wasn't quite over yet. 'I have to make sure he understands,' I told Todd.

'What do you mean?'

'About Grandad, and what I'll do if anything happens to him.'

Todd had listened carefully to everything I told him, and he had understood remarkably well. 'You're going to blackmail him, aren't you?'

'Not for money, no, just to protect my grandad.'

'Of course. That's what I meant.'

'But he has to know that I'm serious, that I'm just as tough as he is.'

I didn't feel tough. I felt like a jelly, one that has just been taken out of the fridge and now its sitting on the kitchen table, wobbling. I wished I could stop shaking.

'You can do it, Rosie. You *are* tough, if you ask me. It's that Mr Sidebottom who should be worried. You've got him over a barrel and he'll have to beg you not to dob him in.'

'I know, but I have to make *him* see that.'

Todd shifted his chair closer and took my hands in his. 'You can do it. And I'm going to help you.'

I was about to ask how in God's name he thought he was going to help me when the mobile trilled its familiar tune. 'Oh shit, it's him!'

It was, too.

'WHAT THE HELL DO YOU THINK YOU'RE DOING?' boomed that familiar voice, now hysterical with rage. 'You've given the ring back, haven't you?'

I couldn't let him rant and rave and build himself into even more of a fury. I had to make a response and somehow get the upper hand. 'It was *her* ring,' I reminded him calmly.

'I warned you. I told you I wanted that ring myself.'

I looked at Todd, who was still leaning close, a kind of support just by being here. He offered a grim smile and even a wink. 'Go for him, Rosie,' he whispered. 'Show him who's the boss.'

It was just enough to get me going. 'Yes, and I know *why* you wanted the ring, as well. You were going to make sure it was never returned to your wife. You were going to cheat the insurance company and make them pay out twenty thousand dollars for a bit of cheap imitation jewellery. The police would be very interested in *that* piece of information.'

'You wouldn't dare. Your grandfather will pay if you go anywhere near them.'

'Oh, I won't, Mr Sidebottom, not as long as Paddy Larkin has an easy time in gaol. If you could threaten him like that then you can damn well make things safe for him instead. And if you don't, then it won't just be the police I tell about your fake ring. The first call I make will be to your wife. I bet she'll be *very* interested to hear that her precious ring has a phoney diamond in it.'

There it was. The gasp down the line that I'd been waiting for. He tried to bluff his way out. 'Go right ahead. That pathetic fool of a jeweller will take the fall. I can always claim he switched the stones.'

'No-one will believe that,' I replied, becoming more confident by the second. 'Everyone knows what Mr Farr is like. He wouldn't dare pull a scam like that on his own. And even if the police fall for it, the lovely Narelle won't. She knows you. She'll send in the divorce lawyers to clean you out.'

That got him. The most vicious blow to a guy like Sidebottom is to threaten his money. His tirade seemed to have waned somewhat, so I kept up the conversation from my end. My shaking had stopped now, I noticed, and as for Todd, he was laughing out loud.

'Now, listen, Mr Sidebottom. Your wife has her ring back now and there's nothing you can do about it. You'd just better hope that she never has it valued by anyone else. Somehow I doubt she'll ever take it off her finger again anyway. As for you, you won't do anything, to me *or* my grandad, because you know exactly what will happen if you do, and let me make it perfectly plain that I'm not the only one who knows what you were up to. It's all over. Goodbye.'

I stabbed the End button. Yes, it was OVER! I flopped back in the director's chair and nearly went over backwards.

'Rosie,' said Todd in a whisper, 'you're amazing.'

'Amazing! I'm a bloody genius. What about another soft drink?' I suggested, handing him my glass.

The drink was cool in my throat, the chairs very comfortable and Todd surprisingly good company, and after a performance like that, I deserved to bask in the glow of his admiration. Actually, I was admiring *him* quietly too. He had been more of a help than he realised. I didn't feel like going home just yet, and he certainly wasn't in any hurry to get rid of me.

We talked for over an hour. What did we talk about? It didn't seem to matter but I liked him more as every minute passed. Chris might be wild and dangerous, with edges that could cut and burn, but Todd was smooth and easy to talk to in a way that I liked just as much. I saw again what a good-looking guy he was — maybe not quite a hunk like Chris Meagher, but he was three years younger and boy, was he cute. Too bad my hormones were looking for something a bit more exciting than cute.

Around five, Mrs Rooney came home with Todd's younger brother and his two noisy younger sisters. She took one look at my skirt and changed her mind about me, but I didn't care. I wasn't caring about much at all by that time. Todd walked me out to the car, and as he stood chivalrously holding the door open for me, I said 'Thanks' for the tenth time. To show that I meant it, I squeezed his hand, and ... oh, what the heck, I stretched up on my toes and kissed him on the cheek.

He looked a bit surprised, but not half as surprised as I looked a few moments later. With a quick glance toward his house, he leaned in close, moving his mouth to my ear while his voice became a whisper. 'You know how I said you looked like Uma Thurman back at The Grove? Well, actually, when I saw you staring through that window, you looked more like Jennifer Lopez.'

I pulled back sharply to find a cheeky gleam in his eye, and he wasn't the least embarrassed to let me see it. '*Especially* in that skirt,' he added, and in case there was any doubt about what he meant, he reached behind me and put his hand firmly on the part that reminded him most of Jennifer Lopez. Then he kissed me just as firmly — and not on the cheek, either.

Oh, boy. The world had suddenly become a different place. This is ridiculous, I told myself. How can a girl let herself be so attracted to two different guys at the same time?

Bloody hormones!

TWENTY-NINE

THE MERC MUST HAVE STARTED itself and automatically jumped into gear, because the next thing I remember was driving away shell-shocked from the Rooneys' house. I rang the salon, but Tracey was closing up and she'd already volunteered to drive Glenda home. I would go round and visit her after dinner and tell her the whole unbelievable story. In the meantime, I let the Mercedes wander wherever it liked around the streets of Prestwidge, feeling like a queen in her royal carriage.

Did it really have a mind of its own, that black Mercedes? Maybe it did, or maybe there was something else at work in its direction-finding. It had taken me to Fergo's garage.

I glanced at the petrol gauge. Yes, it was finally dipping towards empty. I pulled up beside the pump. Darren answered the ring of the bell, but just like last time, as soon as he recognised the Merc he went back into the workshop. Moments later, Christian Meagher emerged.

'How much this time, Ma'am? Three dollars' worth?'

He was full of himself as usual, but then would I be here if he didn't smile at me like that? I sat back silently in the driver's seat and let the pump put him in his place. Thirty-eight dollars' worth.

'I was going to give you a call. There's a rumour going round about who Kenny's working for. Doesn't make any sense, though —'

'Terry Sidebottom,' I cut in smugly.

That took the smirk off his face. 'It's true, then. So what's happened about the ring?'

'All taken care of,' I told him. 'You want to hear about it?'

'Of course. Hey, actually, you can do me a favour. I let a friend have my car for a few hours. You could drop me at his place and save him from having to bring it back.'

He jumped into the passenger seat.

'No bears to keep you company this time,' I said.

'You'll have to do instead,' he responded, smiling like a devil and slipping across the seat much closer than my passengers usually sat.

Oh, boy, the dilemmas a girl can get herself into.

'Where to?' I asked.

He gave me good enough directions to get me started, and with the Mercedes in no particular hurry, I told him how I had returned the ring to Mrs Sidebottom. For once that laconic façade he liked to project slipped rapidly away.

'You're joking,' he said over and over. 'You beat him. The biggest mongrel in Prestwidge, and *you* took him down! Rosie, you're a legend!'

'To a handful of people, maybe. It's not like I can spread the story around.'

'You can trust *me*,' he said, and I knew I could — about that, anyway. There were other areas where the same thing didn't necessarily apply. Take, for instance, the fact that his hand had mysteriously found its way onto my knee.

'Great car,' said Chris for the umpteenth time, as his hand moved just that tiny fraction higher en route to my thigh.

He didn't say any more for a minute or two, and I continued to monitor the upward steady movement. His hand was now at the hem of Glenda's little black skirt, which had ridden up pretty high on my legs as it was. 'I'd *love* to drive it,' he said.

'Don't press your luck,' I cautioned him, with a playful smile that told him he was getting two warnings in one.

'Oh, come on, Rosie. You can trust me with your grandfather's car. I've never driven a Merc.'

'Same as any other car,' I snapped, aware of how disloyal this must sound, and hoping my black taxi would forgive me.

But Chris wasn't giving up that easily. 'It's not far to my mate's place now. Come on, give us a go.'

Yeah, but if I let him drive, would we go straight there? Good question. Did I want to go on a little detour? Um, another good question.

'Your grandad won't mind if you let me drive,' he cooed.

Talk about persistent! He was getting awfully persistent somewhere else, too.

I pulled over to the curb, coming to a halt just ahead of a bus shelter. Chris had a huge grin across his dial, and as soon as the car stopped he had the door open. I watched him climb out and walk round the front of the car, his boots crunching on the grit of the road.

When he reached my side, he realised that I hadn't moved.

'Slide across, Rosie.'

He didn't understand. No, for all that swagger and all his gorgeous looks, what he lacked was that tiny grain of understanding. He didn't understand that this was *my* place behind the wheel and I didn't really want to surrender it.

I pressed lightly down on the accelerator and the Mercedes responded, sweeping past Chris Meagher, who had just enough time to register astonishment on his face. Then I was gone.

I rounded the corner, leaving him to fend for himself — but he was a big boy and there would be a bus along in another twenty minutes or so.

There I was, alone in the car, but somehow it felt like Eric and Janice were in there with me, and Mrs Giastacomo and her husband, even though he wouldn't know where he was, and the Eisenberg sisters, quietly arguing, and over the top of the engine's noise I imagined I could hear Mrs Foat's voice raised in muted triumph.

'Go, Rosie!'